Culp, Judy
The search for justice

THE SEARCH FOR JUSTICE

Other books by Judy and Ronald Culp:

The Search for Truth
The Search for Freedom

THE SEARCH FOR JUSTICE

•

Judy and
Ronald Culp

AVALON BOOKS
NEW YORK

All the characters in this book are fictitious,
and any resemblance to actual persons,
living or dead, is purely coincidental.
Published by Thomas Bouregy & Co., Inc.
160 Madison Avenue, New York, NY 10016

Library of Congress Cataloging-in-Publication Data
Culp, Judy.
The search for justice / Judy and Ronald Culp.
p. cm.
ISBN 978-0-8034-9920-1 (acid-free paper)
I. Culp, Ronald. II. Title.
PS3603.U59S428 2008
813'.6–dc22 2008017393

PRINTED IN THE UNITED STATES OF AMERICA
ON ACID-FREE PAPER
BY HADDON CRAFTSMEN, BLOOMSBURG, PENNSYLVANIA

Our thanks go to family, history, and the Bible,
all of which inspire our imagination.

Chapter One

He held the reins of the plodding, two-horse hired team loosely in his hands and shifted his position on the padded seat of the spring wagon. Gray eyes squinting in the bright sunlight, he tilted his head from side to side to ease stiffening muscles. Catherine, his wife of not yet one year, nodded on the seat beside him, eyes closed. The road stretched into the sun-blasted distance ahead of them. He pushed his hat to the back of his head to allow the warm wind to dry his sweaty brow.

"Long" Tilman Wagner, now forty-five years old but still as lean and hard-muscled as a man half his age, considered himself fortunate. He had fought on the losing side in a war, found nothing to keep him in the South, moved to Texas, and tried to become a cattleman. Sarah, his first wife, died there at the hands of a couple of wandering Indians, leaving Tilman to rear their young son.

He made little time for the boy but, hate-filled, chose instead to ride a dark trail of revenge against renegade Indians. Over time he included outlaws—men of any race—in his revenge, and he rode mostly on the right side of the law. He had scars from those years, and not all of them were on the outside. On the Texas plains, a man sometimes made his own law. Tilman reassured himself that he'd never killed someone who didn't deserve to die.

Somebody had murdered his son, Dan, when the boy was barely twenty years old. Tilman had ridden to Colorado and found the man responsible, then saw him fall under someone else's gun. He took small comfort in that; the man would never do murder again.

In one of those odd turns life seems to take when a man's least expecting it, he'd found a second chance in Colorado. His mind wandered, and, half-smiling, he thought once again that it was odd how the love of a good woman could make a difference in a man. He'd had doubts; he did not trust himself. He had tried to pull away from her, which was a fact. Yet Tilman could not chase Catherine from his thoughts, and so he'd returned to Colorado and married her.

He looked over his shoulder at his newly adopted son, James, curled in sleep among their baggage in the bed of the wagon. Now he had another chance at rearing a boy. But did a man with his past deserve a second chance? Catherine and her Bible-thumping preacher friend assured him it was possible. Maybe so, but did the memories ever go away? Best let the past lie, he reminded himself, for he had been a different sort of man when he did those things. Marriage—well, it was Catherine, he had to admit, not the institution itself—was changing him. Still, he didn't want to lose his edge.

Beside him, Catherine awoke with a start, cleared her throat, arched an aching back, and stretched.

"Hmm," she said. "I thought we'd be there before now. I'd better get used to these long distances." Catherine filled a dipper from the water barrel, drank, and offered some to Tilman.

He wrapped the reins around his right wrist and took the dipper in his left. Her hand brushed his in the exchange of the dipper. He filled his mouth, held the water, swallowed, and commented, "Mighty good."

Catherine shook dust from her traveling dress—the blue plaid now more brown than blue from all the road dust they'd stirred up over the last few days. "I bet I look like I've been storing my clothes in a dustbin." Patting her skirt one last time, Catherine stifled a cough when her hands raised puffs of dust.

"No, ma'am, Mrs. Wagner, you look grand." Tilman gazed fondly at his wife. Turning to James, he called, "Wake up, boy!"

James mumbled sleepily. "I have to go behind a tree," he complained.

"Time to grease that left rear hub anyway," Tilman said. "It's squealing again." Pulling the team to a halt and setting the brake, he climbed down.

"It's so quiet," Catherine commented. "As if there's not a soul in the world but us."

"True. You'd sure be able to hear anybody stirring out here," Tilman answered, looking around. With a brush he slapped grease from a bucket onto the dry wheel hub while James ran behind a clump of scrub oak.

When they were moving on down the road again, Tilman joked with James. "Doesn't all this dust coating everything remind you of when your mom makes those great doughnuts and gets flour everywhere?" Tilman laughed. "Maybe brown flour."

"You're right, Dad, but talking about doughnuts makes me hungry." James' freckles stood out, his fair skin reddened despite the wide-brimmed straw hat his mother made him wear. He fidgeted. As far as he was concerned, he had ridden far enough. "Are we going to get there today?"

"I think we've heard that before," Catherine commented. She pulled a worn telegram from her dark blue crocheted purse, a wedding present from a neighbor in Vista Buena, Colorado. "I just hope we're in time to help, Tilman." She reread the telegram.

> *URGENT YOU HELP STOP DANGER LOSING EVERYTHING STOP COME IF YOU CAN STOP DAVID*

It had been a long and tiring journey by train, stage, and finally in the spring wagon Tilman hired in Socorro. Over the years, the Army and traders had left passable roads across this part of New Mexico Territory, although at times Tilman's usually reliable sense of direction led them jolting across trackless plains, with him insisting all the while that he was not lost. The white officer leading a column of black cavalrymen past their campsite near a mountain stream late the previous afternoon had assured Tilman he was within a day's ride of his destination. The Rio Bonito crossing lay several miles behind them, and he was certain that the foothills rising to meet them were on David Stone's ranch.

Beyond those hills, a tall woman, dress rustling in the warm afternoon wind, stood facing two men.

"I reckon your old man ain't at home. Me and Chunk here," the young man with a black eye patch said, pointing with his thumb at the hefty older rider beside him, "we come to keep you from gettin' too lonesome." With a sly, mirthless smirk, the young man leered. "Ain't that right, Chunk?" As he spoke, he eased down from his saddle and dabbed the reins carelessly over a hitch rail.

Chunk, his dark chin stubble unevenly streaked with brown tobacco juice, curled his lip in what passed for a friendly grin and crossed one leg over the saddle horn, tilted his hat to the back of his head, and said, "That's right, Bob." Chunk coldly eyed Esperanza in anticipation. "I want to see her let that long black hair down."

Esperanza Stone had never seen the two men before. She stood on the front step by the rose garden she patiently nursed in the warm New Mexico climate, her striking dark hair lightly laced with silver. Her smoldering brown eyes observed the two men with loathing and nothing more. She felt their eyes on her. In town men looked as she passed by, she knew, for Esperanza's figure belied the fact that she had given David Stone four children. "You," she snapped at the one-eyed man called Bob. "Don't come any closer. Leave the way you came. I have no use for you here."

Ignoring her, the young man stretched lazily, hitching up his jeans. Clearly, Bob fancied himself a man irresistible to the fairer sex, one accustomed to having his way with women. He looked around, swaggering with bravado, and took a step closer to the shaded area beneath a line of tall poplars in front of the hacienda, saying, "Get that bottle outta my saddlebags, Chunk. I feel a mite of chill in the air."

Sudden movement caught his eye, and he froze at the sight of a double-barreled shotgun's muzzle thrust from the darkness of the open front door. "Well, look what we got here. An old grammaw packing iron! Careful, old gal, that thing might go off and hurt you," he taunted.

Behind him, Bob heard the creak of saddle leather as Chunk shifted his weight, barking a humorless, "Haw!"

A determined-looking Tomasa Lopez, long black dress covering her diminutive, five-foot frame, her gray hair pulled severely into a tight bun under a black veil, also came out onto the wide front step, managing awkwardly to point the heavy shotgun in the direction of the two strangers. She faced the men, trying to steady the long gun. From the set of her mouth, the old woman was obviously toothless, and she was plainly unfamiliar with handling such a weapon, as the rabbit-ear hammers remained uncocked, and her fingers were nowhere near the trigger guard.

Suddenly Esperanza reached out and took the gun from the old woman. Without hesitation, she expertly eared back the hammers. Then the barrels dropped as she squeezed off a blast of lead shot that gouged a hole in the hard-packed dirt at the man's feet and threw up a cloud of dust mixed with gun smoke. Uttering a stunned oath, the one-eyed man staggered backward, not yet certain he was still in one piece. Spooked, his horse lunged backward, and the man barely managed to grab the reins to keep his mount from running away. In the confusion, his brand-new high-crowned Montana peak hat fell under his feet, while the sound of Chunk's derisive laughter burned his ears. This was *not* what Bob had expected to happen!

"Get off our land, and never come back." Esperanza spoke coldly as she aimed at the man's belly. "Or next time I won't fire into the dirt." Aiming just above their heads, Esperanza let fly with a load of buckshot from the other barrel.

"You ain't seen the last of us," the man hissed as he scooped up his now misshapen hat and swung into the saddle.

Tomasa stepped around Esperanza, both hands grasping a huge nickel-plated Smith & Wesson .44-caliber Russian-model pistol.

"Look out!" Chunk shouted. "Now that old crone's got a six-shooter!"

With both eyes squeezed shut, Tomasa fired a shot in the general direction of the two men, who turned their horses and spurred hard to get out of range. Cursing about the useless, evil men of this world who would dare intrude here, Tomasa staggered backward from the gun's recoil and dropped the unwieldy weapon into the dust. Next she pulled a dangerous-looking butcher knife from the folds of her apron and pointed it at the fleeing men. The woman was a walking arsenal!

"Crazy old bat!" the skinnier rider shouted as their horses leaped over one of the *acequias,* the irrigation ditches that watered the nearby hay fields. From the safety of a hundred yards' distance they circled, trying to decide whether to leave or try one more time.

Esperanza snorted in disgust and started back to the house for more shotgun shells.

Chapter Two

The gunshot sounded from up ahead of the wagon trail and echoed from the hills across the valley. It appeared there were in fact other souls besides them in the world, Tilman reflected, and one of them had a gun. Then came a second shot. Then silence.

Catherine turned to him, worried, and placed a hand on his arm. "That was a shotgun. Could be there's a bird hunter out there."

Tilman motioned for her to be silent, and his free hand dropped to slip the hammer thong from his belted pistol. He saw the apprehension in Catherine's eyes, knowing she didn't like it when he strapped on his gun. However, Tilman's caution came from the knowledge that recent range wars had attracted some of the worst gunmen and killers in the West to this part of New

Mexico Territory. Raw greed and lawlessness had cost many lives, and there was every reason to believe the rampaging was not over. Only a fool would ride out here and not be ready for anything, and Tilman certainly hadn't lived this long by acting a fool.

"Just a precaution," he assured his wife. "I don't think we have anything to worry about." He urged the tired animals to move along. "James, you be on the lookout. Stay behind your mother. If you see anybody following us, you sing out, you understand?"

"Yes, sir." James moved to the back end of the wagon and settled himself down so that he could peer over the tailgate. He imagined himself the stalwart hero in a dime novel, looking over a boulder for hostiles intent on doing mischief. His mother slid across the seat to be closer to Tilman.

When the third shot popped, Tilman knew that this time the sound came from a pistol. Catherine's hands grasped the seat rail as the wagon bounced along on the rocky road. Cresting a low ridge brought an unforgettable, panoramic view of a large, fortlike, Spanish-style home with the outbuildings of a working ranch nestled in a wind-rippled sea of blue grama grass on the southern slope of the hills in the near distance. Tilman was certain that this must be their destination, the ranch belonging to his brother-in-law. Miles to the east was a wide valley before a backdrop of a steep, dun-colored mountain. The blue sky was clear, with only the occasional billowing, dark-bottomed cloud. At any other time he might appreciate such a beautiful picture, but trouble lay ahead, for the gunshots had come from that direction. Tilman held the team at a run. A quick glance to his left revealed Catherine cradling his big Winchester rifle, ready to help if needed. Catherine was something else. No fussing or fainting or anything. Just as calm as could be. He was indeed a lucky man.

As they drew closer, Tilman could make out two men on horseback near two figures—women—standing in the shade of a line of tall trees. It looked like some sort of standoff.

Down at the house, Tomasa touched Esperanza's elbow and then pointed with her chin toward the road. "*Mira*—look there!"

Esperanza saw a spring wagon with several people in it, horses running hard toward the house on the once well-kept lane. She cradled the shotgun under her right arm as Tomasa hid the knife in the folds of her skirt. Esperanza raised a hand to shade her eyes, squinting to see the visitors. "Could that be . . . ?"

Across the distance came the sound of a man's shouted warning.

"Company, Chunk!" Bob yelled.

The two riders wheeled their horses and spurred off in the opposite direction, two clouds of dust following them.

Tilman slowed the team and brought the wagon to a halt in the circular drive in front of the house, the horses dancing in excitement. He climbed down and grabbed the harness to settle the team. The two women carefully studied the newcomers.

The shotgun rose to point at Tilman. The woman—Esperanza, he assumed—smoldered with anger. He could see that here was no timid mouse of a woman frightened of her own shadow. She stood straight, dark eyes flashing, only the color in her cheeks betraying her emotions as she looked at him over the barrels of the shotgun. There was a regal air about her that defied the time and place. Her black hair pulled back in a matronly bun glistened in the afternoon sun, the silver streak in the front only adding to her beauty.

"Esperanza?" Catherine said as James helped his mother step down from the wagon. "It's me, Catherine Wagner, and this is my husband, Tilman, and our son, James." She faltered under the woman's stern gaze. "I'm David's sister. I—"

"Oh, *perdón.* Pardon me, Catherine. Tilman. James." Esperanza Stone wearily dropped the gun to her side, evident relief washing over her. "I knew you would come. Those men . . ." She paused, visibly gathered her wits, and calmed her breathing. Quickly she went to each of her guests, hugging them in welcome. Her prayers had been answered. Help, she was certain, had arrived. "I hoped you would get here in time. I didn't know where else to turn."

Tilman eyes searched the near distance where the two riders had disappeared. "I take it David is not here?"

A nod from Esperanza answered the question. Tilman

touched the brim of his hat, saying, "I think it's a good idea for me to go see that those men don't circle around and get the drop on us." He bent to pick up a Smith & Wesson pistol from the ground. "You may need this."

At Catherine's sharp intake of breath, Tilman quickly added, "If I see them, I'll just talk with them. Do you have any idea where they came from, Esperanza?"

"No, Tilman. I've never seen them before. But many of the ranches have hired new men, and some are not as polite as others." Her shoulders dropped in resignation. "You understand?"

Tilman turned to James, who stood by his mother's side. "Son, lead the team around to the stable, and make sure the horses are taken care of, please. I'll need a fresh horse, Esperanza."

"Of course." She issued some instructions in rapid Spanish to an ancient and bent little man who had appeared from behind her. The man hurried off.

"It'll go faster if I give him a hand," Tilman said.

"Be careful," Catherine called.

"Here," Esperanza said. "Come in and get out of the sun. Let me welcome you properly." She turned to the older woman. "Tomasa, bring cool water from the *olla*." She turned back to Catherine as the old woman shuffled into the dark recesses of the large adobe hacienda. "Sorry, that was Tomasa. She was my *dueña*—my chaperone—when I grew up, and she still looks after me as if I am a young girl." She took Catherine's hands and stood looking at her. "It has been a long time in coming, no?" She hugged Catherine once more and stepped back. "Welcome, my sister. You are indeed all welcome to our home." Esperanza ushered her guests inside.

Chapter Three

Tilman rode off, casting about until he found the men's trail. It was easy to follow, for the men expected no pursuit and therefore had made no effort to conceal their direction or tracks. Nor did they appear to be in any kind of hurry. Wary, lest he stumble onto the men unprepared, Tilman drew his rifle from the saddle scabbard the old man called Santiago had supplied. It was the gun he'd bought down in Mesilla, a Winchester Model 1876, chambering a big .45-75 cartridge, the 350-grain .45-caliber lead slug pushed along by seventy-five grains of black powder. The gun was reliable and had served him well, for it packed considerable stopping power at distances well beyond five hundred yards. Tilman had no idea what to expect, but, bracing the curved and heavy brass-framed butt of the stock on his right thigh, he wanted to be ready for anything.

He had followed the trail for an hour or more and was climbing into a forested area when he caught the smell of cigarette smoke on the breeze. *Close!* He reined up, almost blundering into the two men among the trees. Did they know he was following them? Had they stopped to wait in ambush for the unknown rider behind them? He had no fear of the kind of men who would bully women. He'd dealt with such before. Besides, he had plenty of cartridges, if they wanted to take it to gunplay.

He climbed out of the saddle and saw his horse looking in the direction the men had taken. Placing a hand over his horse's nose to keep him from nickering a call to the other horses, Tilman led the now quiet animal to a clump of green grass. He loosened the girth and left the horse munching contentedly. Carefully Tilman made his way closer to the men.

He had not gone far when a windowless log cabin came into sight, partially dug into the side of a gentle slope surrounded by scrubby oaks. Probably some rancher's line shack.

Two saddled horses, tails swishing at flies, stood in a pole corral that joined one side of the cabin. Two men, one wearing a black patch over his right eye, sat on logs near a circle of rocks surrounding the cold ashes of a fire pit. They were passing a bottle between them, smoking and talking. The men hadn't the look of working cowboys. Drifters, they were, perhaps, or a couple of cheap guns. Neither of them looked exactly prosperous.

"When are we goin' back down there?" the hefty man whined.

"Let me think on it," the younger man growled back at him, his good eye flashing angrily. "I didn't expect Señora Stone to have company calling today."

"She's a good-looking woman, but she's too proud. I reckon I'll take her down a notch or two."

"Yeah? You'd better make sure that old gal with her don't get the drop on you, or you'll end up like me." With a snort, he added, "Why don't you take that old 'un? She's more like the gals I've seen you with!"

"Now, don't talk like that. Naw, I'll just knock the old hag on the head first."

Tilman stepped into view. "No sudden moves, boys, and keep those hands where I can see 'em," he said.

The young man's good eye narrowed, the whiskey dulling his judgment. Tilman guessed this one would try to draw, even though the Winchester was leveled at his chest. "Go ahead. Reach for it. If you think you can clear leather before this slug lets daylight through you, then give it a try."

The young man shook his head. "Naw. I'll not try it."

"That's the first smart thing you've done all day. Now, you ease that left hand down, and unbuckle that gun belt." When the young man's weapon fell to the ground, Tilman had the other man do the same.

"Are you the law?" the older man asked. "You got a badge?"

"What business do you two have at Stone's?" Tilman asked.

"Are you one of the Regulators?" the heavier man asked.

"I'm not part of the range wars around here. Now, answer my question," Tilman barked.

"What you talking about? Who's this Stone?" the young man snarled.

With two quick strides forward, Tilman slammed his gun butt into the man's chin, knocking him to the ground, where he sprawled, unmoving, in the dirt, jaw already swelling and turning a dark purple.

"Easy there, fellow," the older man pleaded in a quaking voice, hands up as if to ward off any blow from the big, angry intruder facing him.

"Are you going to answer me?" Tilman demanded. "Or do you want a taste of the same thing your friend got?"

"We was just looking for a little fun," the man croaked in fear. "We seen that Mex woman in town and thought maybe she'd be right for a little fandango."

"What else?"

"Honest, mister. That's all it was."

"You two from around here?"

"Just passin' through, ridin' the grub line, lookin' for a little work."

"Listen to this. You know what's good for you, you both keep on riding. If I catch you on this land again, you're going under. You get me?"

The one-eyed man Tilman had struck let out a moan and reached up to feel his throbbing face. "Oh," he mumbled through clenched teeth, "my jaw's broke." He spat tooth fragments into the palm of his right hand and held them up to his face, goggling with his one good eye. "And you broke my teeth too."

Tilman tapped the muzzle of his Winchester on the man's forehead. "A broke jaw's better than waking up dead." He turned out the men's horses and sent them running with a slap across the rump and a couple of shots fired into the air. He turned to the men. "Give me those boots."

"What?"

"Shuck 'em. You're drifting by way of shank's mare and unshod from now on."

"That ain't right, mister!" the older one protested.

"You're still able to draw breath. Be glad for that. Now get going."

Tilman gathered up their guns and boots and rode away, leaving the two to their complaining and protesting, mincing walk on tender feet.

Riding back to the Stone place, Tilman thought about what he'd done. Catherine would be shocked. She'd say he ought to feel some remorse, but that was crowded out by the thought of what those men would have done to Esperanza had he not showed up when he did. He had no doubt that the drifters would have had their way and shown no mercy. Once again Tilman thought about how near the surface his old ways could be found. Would he ever leave those ways behind?

Chapter Four

On the ride back to the house, Tilman turned aside at the sight of a flock of buzzards circling in the air. Many more hopped about awkwardly on the ground, fighting over several cattle carcasses. The dead animals lay near a spring-fed water tank, and as he neared it, Tilman saw more buzzards rise squawking from a coyote and two antelope. *Poison!* Somebody had dumped poison into the tank. Whatever was going on here had taken a serious turn. That explained the telegram David Stone had sent to his sister.

Tilman turned over the incident with the two drifters in his mind. He couldn't let it go and felt uneasy. What was their tie to the poisoned water tank? Why had he so quickly accepted their protested innocence? He ought to know better than that. It was a shame he hadn't passed by the dead cattle before he found the two men. Something was not right about those so-called drifters, and he felt foolish. It was not like him to make such a mistake.

As the afternoon sun slipped into the edge of the day, Tilman returned to the ranch. The hacienda sat square and large, built around a courtyard that Tilman admired as he rode down the hillside. Large windows opened onto the yard, enabling breezes to flow through the house. It was a building that had been made to last. Catherine had said that the main house had been in Esperanza's family for over sixty years. As a young man, Catherine's brother had come here, met and fallen in love with the land and Esperanza, and never returned to his family back east. Catherine, a child at the time, had corresponded with David and his family, but they hadn't seen each other since he left home.

When he had turned his horse over to old Santiago at the stables, Tilman paused, puzzled by the lack of working ranch hands on such a large place. It was odd that he'd seen only the one elderly, worn out *vaquero.* He went in the back door, finding himself in an enormous kitchen, where James sat by Tomasa, eating. The boy's stomach was bottomless.

"Here, Dad. Have one of these. They're great."

Tilman popped a small treat into his mouth, then licked his fingers. "What am I eating?"

"Empanadas, Señor Wagner. *Muy sabroso."*

"They are small pies we fill with jelly, meat, or fruit. Tomasa not only wields a gun, she is also a wonderful cook." Esperanza and Catherine slipped into the kitchen behind Tilman. Tomasa looked on with approval as he helped himself to a handful of the small pastries. Catherine came to Tilman and gave him a quick kiss on the cheek. "I'm glad you're back safe."

Tilman sent James outside and sat at the table with his wife and sister-in-law. The women listened quietly while he told what he had done and what he had seen. "Where is David?" he asked. "And who were those men, and what did they want? Where is everyone else?"

"Tilman, we've just arrived!" Catherine chided her husband.

"No, no," Esperanza said, placing her hand over Catherine's. "Now is as good a time as any. You must know if you are to assist us." Turning to Tilman, she answered, "Our land is very valuable these days. Many of the men who are coming into this territory from the United States want to claim this for their own. We own the land on both sides of the river, and water is especially important here." Esperanza stood, then paced, as she talked. "Small 'accidents' happen. At first David thought they were just that. Accidents. But"—she stopped, trying to collect her thoughts—"lately they have been more serious and more frequent. We are losing cattle—the herd David rounded up for the last buyer was stolen."

"The entire herd was rustled?" Tilman asked.

"Yes," Esperanza said. "The men rounded up almost fifteen hundred cattle. The rustlers killed two of our men, old Bernal and his son Domingo. Somebody poisoned one of our wells—we found white crystal powder spilled on the ground. The men say it was strychnine—

you know, the poison they use in wolf and coyote bait. Last week we found that some of our cattle had been shot, and now you tell me that another tank has been poisoned." She sat back down. After a moment, she continued. "The five young *vaqueros*—not the *viejos,* the old ones who have been with the family for years—the men David hired to move the herd, they have been frightened away. Young men today have no honor." She sighed.

"We have a few men," she continued, "but they are spread out over the range, trying to find strays and anything else that may have escaped the rustlers, so we can make a small herd before it is too late and we are ruined." Esperanza straightened her back. "Do you understand?"

"Yes," Tilman answered. "Clearly, somebody wants you off this land and will stop at nothing to get his way. Those men this afternoon, they were sent here to rough you up and get you to leave."

"They would stoop to that?" Esperanza asked.

"And worse. I shouldn't have let them off so easily. Next time I see them, I won't."

"Tilman, please," Catherine said, touching Tilman's clenched fist on the table. "You're not that way anymore."

"It will be fine. God will provide. See?" Esperanza put her hand on Catherine's shoulder. "He has sent the three of you to help us in our time of need." Esperanza gestured with her other hand. "Now I must tell you more. David went to check on our horses up in the high pasture last week. It is not far, and I expected him to be home by now. It is probably nothing, but I am afraid something may have happened, and he may be hurt.

He loves his Spanish barbs, but he never stays away without letting us know where he is."

"Did he go alone?"

"Yes. He was worried, for those horses are like his pets. I know my husband, and this isn't like him. Juan Javier, our oldest son, has been away, selling some of our other horses, but he should be home tonight. When he returns, I will send him to look for his father."

"I'll go with him." Tilman stood and stretched, his brief rest awakening in him every ache and pain of the long days of travel. Catching Catherine's eye, he paused. "For now, I believe it's time for us to rest and get cleaned up."

"Of course. What was I thinking?" Esperanza apologized.

Tilman helped Catherine up as well. "I'm travel weary, and I know Catherine needs a nap." He turned to Esperanza. "Don't worry. We'll get to the bottom of this."

Esperanza watched the two as they went to their quarters. She hoped that Tilman Wagner could help before something bad happened. Tomasa, ever superstitious, had seen an owl circle the house in broad daylight two days ago and swore it meant trouble. Although Esperanza didn't believe the woman's tales, the thought still made her shiver.

Chapter Five

"These rooms are so cool and comfortable, don't you agree?" The high-ceilinged rooms were square and spacious. Overhead, six massive, peeled ponderosa-pine beams supported a whitewashed mat of reeds or saplings, providing a sense of openness.

"The hacienda is very old, but it certainly is solidly built," Catherine continued. "Mateo—that's Esperanza's father—had a builder from Mexico City come to design the newer buildings. I remember David's writing to my family and telling us about it when I was younger." The two guests admired the workmanship. "A home like this one will last for many years."

Catherine went to unpack, only to find that Esperanza had already sent someone to do that task for her and put their belongings in a large, ornately carved, dark armoire. The piece of furniture, nearly ten feet tall, had a lovely, circular mirror inside one door that made it very easy to see what several days on the road had done to her and her new outfit.

"Why didn't you tell me I look as if I walked all the way here?" She laughed as she went to the washstand, where a large pitcher filled with cool water sat in a wide bowl. After pouring water into the bowl, she splashed some onto her face and toweled off. "Esperanza must think her dust-lady of a sister-in-law never bathes."

"A dust-lady? Hardly, Catherine." Tilman pulled her to him, dust and all. "You are beautiful, and your joy shines through all that dirt." Tilman sneezed as Catherine's hair tickled his nose.

With a knock on the door, one of the young girls who worked in the house stuck her head into the room. Working with another girl, giggling and whispering, she soon had a high-backed metal tub in place behind a colorful, hand-painted room divider. Relaying buckets of hot water, the girls quickly prepared a bath for Catherine.

"This must be heaven!" Catherine laid out clean clothes on the bed and disappeared behind the screen.

Kicking off his boots, Tilman stretched out on the bed. From behind the screen came a sigh of pleasure as Catherine luxuriated in the hot water.

"Catherine," he said, "all those things Esperanza talked about—the poisoned wells, the shootings? Those aren't coincidences. They don't just happen. Somebody is making trouble, and we don't know why."

"You always say," Catherine's said in a sleepy voice, "that you don't believe in coincidences."

"Our being here," Tilman answered. "That's no coincidence either. We're here for a reason."

No answer.

"Hey, don't fall asleep in there, woman. We didn't come all this way for you to drown in the bathtub!"

"Don't worry. I can swim."

"Holler if you get in over your head." He chuckled.

"Tilman Wagner, behave yourself."

Sometimes doubt crept into Tlman's mind, and today's events were troubling. Memories surfaced from his past, when he rode a rough trail. He'd broken that man's jaw today almost as a reflex. What if the fellow was what he'd said, nothing more than a drifter? He wouldn't be the first man to get a few drinks into him and let his mouth get him into trouble. But there was dirt being done to the Stone family—Catherine's and now his family—and he would help however he could.

Chapter Six

As Esperanza waited for her husband at the ranch, in the distant hills at the far reaches of David Stone's land, Chunk checked his carbine one last time. "It don't seem right to me that that man deserves that high-strung woman back at that ranch. Do you think so, Bob?" Chunk took a swallow from the bottle that was never far from his side. "Guess the boss wants this done now, and I'd just as soon do it and be on my way as well. This place is starting to bother me." He turned to Bob. "You sure that's Stone?"

The other man nodded. "There he is," Bob said through his wrapped, lumpy, sore jaw. "That's Stone."

Both men peered around a jumble of granite rocks. Chunk raised his carbine and sighted down the barrel. "Feller"—he spoke to the man who appeared in his sights—"you got something the boss wants, so I hope you've made peace with your Maker." He thumbed back the hammer, smelling the gun oil on the sun-warmed metal. "Hey, Bob, I bet I can hit him from here."

"Put that thing down, Chunk," Bob muttered through clenched teeth. "It's too far. I ain't so sure you can. I want to get closer. If you miss, we'll never catch him. We won't get paid, and the boss'll be fit to be tied."

"Yeah, an' you won't get that fifty dollars to pay for that sombrero you and your hoss trampled."

"Hush up." Bob's jaw was really starting to ache again. He grabbed Chunk's bottle and took a gulp, hoping to kill the pain. The fiery liquor burned when it hit the unhealed cuts and broken teeth inside his mouth. He'd find and take care of that big fellow who'd laid him low like this. One day, he sure would. When his jaw quit hurting. "Let's get over there and come up behind him."

Chunk had no eye for ground, so the hiding place he had chosen was poorly sited. They'd have to move, and that was risky, for if Stone saw them, the game was up.

Tall piñon were sparse where David Stone sat his horse. The spring grass in the high pasture was lush; a nearby stream provided plenty of water, and the herd of colorful horses grazed peacefully, sleek and healthy. With satisfaction, he noted that several of the mares would soon be foaling. A sorrel gelding raised his head high, nickered, and David's horse answered.

Up here, with only the sounds of the cool wind in the pines and a vocal pair of flitting meadowlarks to break the silence under the clear blue sky, his troubles seemed far away. David turned his face into the breeze and filled his lungs. It was time for him to break camp and return home. Esperanza would be worried if he stayed up here too long. Nagging doubts came afresh, because going home meant facing some unpleasant facts. His younger son had run off again. He couldn't make that beef contract. Rustlers constantly deviled him and ran off his cowboys. But at least he still had this land, his home, and his horses.

"Lucky for us," Bob whispered to Chunk as both men drew pistols, "we can come up downwind of that highfalutin feller. Looks like he's taking a siesta in his saddle." The whiskey had dulled some of his pain.

Seconds later a grunt of breath exploded from David Stone's lungs as a violent force knocked him heavily from his saddle, his horse shying away from the smell of blood. As he lay in the tall grass, hot, sharp, burning pain spread from his right side. "Oh," he moaned, "what was that?" The bright sunshine dimmed, darkness closed in, and then came black silence. Nothing.

"Whoo-eee! I told you I'd get him!" Chunk shouted as the sound of their fusillade of gunshots echoed from the hills.

"Fool." Bob muttered. "It was my shot that hit him." The two bushwhackers stood over David Stone's bleeding body.

"He's done for." Chunk laughed. "Now let's round up them hosses. Boss said he'd give us a twenty-dollar bonus if we bring 'em in."

Chapter Seven

Juan Javier had returned home long after Tilman and Catherine retired for the evening. Tilman met the elder Stone son when the family gathered for breakfast the following morning. Juan Javier said nothing, but his face showed plainly that he resented having to have an outsider ride with him to seek his father. He was not very talkative during the meal, which Tilman took to mean the young man felt he didn't need someone he'd never met before today to go with him. However, Esperanza gently insisted, and Tilman concluded that here was an iron-willed woman who would not stand for any back talk from her son once she'd made up her mind.

The two men rode out in the predawn chill of a high plains summer morning, the stars fading as the eastern horizon showed a pale line of light. The riders made an unlikely pair. Tilman, a tall, lean, wide-shouldered man wearing denim jeans and high-topped Texas-star boots, also wore a short leather vest over a homespun shirt and a worn, wide-brimmed, high-crowned hat. Tilman also wore a belted .45 Colt pistol that showed some use.

Though not as tall as Tilman, Juan Javier sat ramrod-straight in the saddle, a muscular young man with the black hair and olive skin of his Hispanic mother's side of the family. He wore a short jacket over a white shirt tucked into dark woolen trousers that flared over his boots. Juan Javier, who had watched silently as Tilman buckled on the Colt, never carried a gun.

Catherine and Esperanza sat in the courtyard, sipping hot, thick, sweet chocolate with cinnamon, in the Mexican tradition, from earthenware mugs.

"I am so glad you and Tilman are here. Things have gotten worse this past year. I don't know how to explain." Esperanza halted, unsure how to proceed. "It hasn't been an easy time." She sighed, her aristocratic hands tightly holding the mug. "It seems that all want what we have. The Mexicans from the south and the white men from the east."

"But this is your land. David wrote me several years ago that your father had the Spanish land grant his family received from the king of Spain in the late 1700s. He said that the surveyor general confirmed his ownership, and then David recorded everything in both your names."

Esperanza tried to explain. "I know all this, but there is something that is not right happening here. It is too much coincidence. There are too many happenings that make no sense."

Catherine sensed a deep sadness in the woman. "What about Cam? Why isn't he here helping Juan Javier and David? I am afraid it makes no sense. Where is he, by the way?"

With a revealing shrug of her shoulders, Esperanza answered. *"Dios sabe solamente*—God only knows, Catherine. I don't. He is probably either gambling, drinking, or in one of those places with loose women. We haven't seen him in over six months. He may be in Tascosa. It is an evil town, but our younger son seems to like it very much."

"Why?"

"I have no answers. Cam is a beautiful man, but he is a lost soul. He is drawn to those places as a moth to a flame. The devil has a hold on him that is stronger than any of our prayers, and that we do not understand. Nothing has ever been enough for him. He has broken his father's heart. David is a good man, and he can't understand what drives Cam. I don't either, if truth be told, but he is our son."

The seriousness of the moment vanished as James rounded a corner of the house, shouting with glee. "Mom! Come see the horse that I get to ride while I'm here!" James' freckles stood out, from both the days traveling in the sun and sheer excitement. Catherine and Esperanza followed him as he grabbed their hands and took them to where a handsome bay horse stood at a hitching post. "This is Rojo. Ain't he great, Mom?"

"*Isn't,* James, and, yes, he is." Catherine turned to the man, bent by years of hard work, holding the horse's reins. "I saw you when we arrived—"

"This is Felipe Santiago, Catherine. He is a *vaquero* and has been with my family always." Esperanza placed a patrician hand on Felipe's sleeve. "He runs the stables for us."

The older man, years of sun and hard work etched into skin lined and dark, beamed at his mistress with unabashed affection. "My father worked for Doña Esperanza's father as I work for her."

"Well, James will be your friend forever. That's for sure, Señor Santiago." Catherine smiled as her son stood by the dark horse. "James hated to leave his pony in Colorado and will be happy to ride again."

"Rojo was Señor Cam's horse when he lived here. He misses the company of a young boy, so it will be *bueno* for them both."

James and Felipe led the horse away as enticing smells of beef and tortillas and beans drew the two women toward the kitchen.

"Our youngest daughter is in school at the convent in Socorro but will be here this weekend, and you will meet her then."

"The picture you sent last year showed a beautiful young lady."

"Thank you. She too is aware of how pretty she is. She draws young men the way honey draws bees. I hoped the convent would settle her, but I am not too sure. The Krells, our neighbors," she said, nodding her head to the north, "are good, honest people. Their son, Walter, and our daughter, Beatriz, have been slowly dancing around a courtship for the last year or two. I don't know. Graciela, our oldest, was always so quiet and reserved, but Beatriz has been a challenge since the day she was born."

As the sun rode high in the sky, Tilman broke the silence. "My son—he's dead now—had a horse like this one I'm riding. Bought him from an Indian." Tilman didn't mind silence, but his curiosity was piqued.

"We breed these horses," Juan Javier said, leaning forward and patting the neck of the unusual silver dapple he rode, "my father and I."

"These are sort of like Indian ponies I've seen but different. What do you call this breed?"

"Spanish barbs. Their line goes back to Arabia, and they came to New Spain with the *conquistadores* of old. The Indians took them for their own. Americans from back east brought their favorite horses into the West, and so the Spanish have now almost disappeared," Juan Javier explained, "but for those bred by my father and a few men like him. An awkward man in the saddle is made into a graceful, sure rider on a horse such as this. The barbs are smart, quick, and good for working stock."

"Can they run?"

"Can they run? My brother, whom you have not met, wins many races on our horses."

Odd, Tilman thought. Why didn't he say his brother's name?

"You will see as well when we reach the trail to the

high pastures," Juan Javier continued. "These animals are dependable, very sure-footed on bad trails. Come," Juan Javier said, "see what they can do."

He touched his spurs to his horse, and a surprised Tilman found himself following Juan Javier as their mounts fell into a ground-eating running walk, shifting then to a rapid road pace, and then long strides opening to a surprisingly fast dead run. A mile down the trail, Juan Javier slowed so the men could talk as they rode side by side. "Do you see?"

"If they handle the trail up there," Tilman said, pointing at the mountains rising before them, "I'm sold!"

As the men rode into the morning, Juan Javier became a bit more talkative. Tilman guessed Juan Javier to be in his late twenties and downright eager to talk about Patricia, his wife, and their young sons.

"Do you like ranching with your father? Is that what you want to do?" They rode at a slower pace. "My son didn't want the kind of life I led when he was younger. All he saw was what I had become. After my wife was killed, I wore my hate like a badge of honor, and I was not a man to take time for raising a son." Tilman practically stopped the horse. "I wish I had listened to him when I had the chance, but I was too busy looking to get revenge for his mother's death. He was gone before I had the chance to make it up to him. But"—he picked up the pace—"I think he knew I'd gone full circle, and I hope he's forgiven me." Tilman compressed his lips into a tight, mirthless smile. "Enough about me. How about you? What do you want to do?"

"I want to know more about breeding horses and cattle. I studied for one year at the university in Texas, but Papá needed me here."

Tilman listened to what the young man said and to what he didn't say as well. Where talk of his wife and sons brought animation and ready smiles to Juan Javier's face, his voice was now touched with—what? Bitterness? Was the young man ambitious but resentful because he had had to cut short his studies and come back home?

Tilman said. "Do you live nearby?"

"Yes, we live in the *achosa*—here in the Territory you Americans call it a *chosey,* an old camp house. My grandfather's father constructed it when the king of Spain gave him the land here. The *achosa* was where he lived in the years before many adobe bricks were made, many piñon cut, and logs dressed so the big house could be built. My wife and I are very happy to live there."

Then it was as if a door closed. Juan Javier had revealed enough. "What about you, Tilman Wagner? My mother explained that you are the husband of my father's sister, and you are here to help my father. Why is it that he needs your help when I am here with him?"

"I'm not sure," Tilman answered honestly. "Catherine and I married only a short time ago, and we came when we got your father's telegram, asking us for help."

"I don't understand. What kind of help?"

Tilman looked directly at Juan Javier. "I was hoping you might shed some light on things for me."

"I confess, I did not know my father sent a telegram," Juan Javier said, clearly irked that his father did not trust him enough to tell him what he was doing with ranch business. "Nor do I know of what trouble he wrote."

"Rustlers, for sure. You don't say much about your brother Cam. He can help you and your father, can't he?"

Juan Javier snorted, "Ha! He is no help. I have to do it all."

"Why?"

"What?"

"Why do you have to do it all?" Tilman asked. "Did your father *ask* you to, or did you just take it all on yourself?"

"I think I do not wish to talk about this with you." They rode quietly for several moments.

Tilman looked ahead, watching for trouble. "Actually, I don't know if it was your mother or your father who wanted us to come."

"Perhaps he will explain to both of us when we meet him today."

The talk was at an end. The trail steepened.

The sun was nearing its zenith in the clear skies as the men rode into a pocket valley high above the plains. The valley floor was bordered by a thick stand of pine trees and covered with lush green grass. A lone black bear at the edge of the trees reared to his hind legs, sniffed the air, and squinted at the intruders before he dropped to all fours to resume his search for grubs under the rotting bark of a deadfall near a sagging picket shed. It was quiet—too quiet for a valley full of horses and men.

"Where are the horses?" Juan Javier exclaimed, trying not to show alarm. "And my father?"

Tilman looked around the valley for any trace of life or activity. Juan Javier circled in one direction while Tilman went in the other. The sun was in Tilman's face, and his horse almost stepped on the inert figure in the tall grass by a dead pine tree. "Juan Javier! Come here!"

Chapter Eight

"It's Papá!" Juan Javier said as he jumped off his horse and knelt beside Tilman.

"He's been shot," Tilman said, "but he's still alive—barely. We've got to get him back to the house." Tilman poured water from his canteen onto his bandana and pressed it to David's gray, colorless face. He saw the likeness to Catherine as he looked at David Stone for the first time. Here was another grim reminder of how fragile life was. Catherine loved her brother even though they lived so far apart and hadn't seen each other for many years. Tilman's first thought was for Catherine, how she would hurt if David were dead. Dried blood caked the man's lower back. A bullet hole, puffy and black, was now almost crusted shut.

"An old man used to run sheep up here. His *carreta*—a two-wheeled cart—was left behind the shed after he died. I'll see if it's still there." Juan Javier bounded into the saddle and spurred his horse toward the shed, sending the complaining bear deeper into the woods.

There were a couple of old blankets in the shed, and Juan Javier shook them out to be sure they held no scorpions or other unwanted guests. They were able to put David in the cart without starting the bleeding again, and they wrapped him in the blankets. Juan Javier's horse shied when Tilman rigged a makeshift harness but soon settled down to pull the cart. Tilman tied his horse to the back of the cart and stood in the bed to drive, as the seat was missing.

"I told him he should not ride out alone," Juan Javier said aloud, tears now streaming down his face. "I knew we should have brought the remuda down sooner."

"I think that whoever shot your father probably took the horses and ran off, so we'd best get him off this mountain." Tilman looked around. "I don't think they're still here, but we need take no chances."

Horse thieves might have come upon David alone up here, Tilman thought, taking him by surprise. Could this be a vendetta or a blood feud? Was someone sent here to find and kill David Stone? Who knew he was riding up here? Was there a spy on the ranch? It was a bad wound, and David's survival was chancy at best.

Tilman was left with his thoughts as they made their slow journey back to the ranch, Juan Javier cradling his father's head while David Stone hovered near death.

Near dawn the next day a rooster was crowing when Dr. Tom Clark, the contract surgeon from nearby Fort Stanton, stepped aside to allow Esperanza into the room where her husband lay sleeping.

Pulling the door closed behind him, Clark said to Tilman, "That's a tough man in there. The wound bled a lot, but it looks worse than it was. The bullet bounced off his ribs, cracked 'em, and tore off a big chunk of meat as it went out his front. Lying in that field ought to have killed him, but it didn't. The ride here in the back of that cart should have finished him, but he's still here. I think he's going to make it."

"We're much obliged, Doctor," Tilman said quietly in the shadows from a kerosene lamp. Fatigue had drained him. It had been a long, long day and a longer night. When he and Juan Javier got the cart to the ranch, one of the *vaqueros* left for Fort Stanton to get the Army doctor, who arrived more quickly than Tilman had believed to be possible. Overworked, underpaid, and doing a demanding job for the government, Army doctors also saw to the needs of the local citizens when necessary.

That evening, Esperanza drew the men and Catherine into the parlor. "Tilman, I want you and Juan Javier to ride to Tascosa to get Cam. He needs to know about his father, and I think that is maybe where he is."

"It will do no good, Mamá."

"Juan Javier, please. For me."

Tilman saw the iron will asserting itself once again. Juan Javier too knew the outcome. "We'll leave in the morning, Esperanza. If Cam is there, we'll bring him home. You have my word."

Juan Javier looked at Tilman. "You don't know my brother."

"Well, it looks like I'm about to meet him." He turned to Catherine. "Let's call it a night. We'll ride in the morning."

Chapter Nine

One of the saloons by the edge of town sported a gaudy sign advertising to all arrivals the FIRST CHANCE SALOON on one side and, for those departing the town, the LAST CHANCE SALOON on the other.

Freighters and cowboys were common sights on the streets of the small Texas panhandle cattle town of Tascosa, and few attracted the eye. Men struggling to make do on small ranches, their wives in faded calico, work-worn and big-eyed at the wonders of the town, appeared often enough but passed unnoticed down the dusty, windblown streets flanked by false-fronted stores, lager beer and whiskey saloons with fading paint, a couple of banks, a hotel, and a restaurant. Town dogs, sleeping in the shade, hardly bothered to bark at such ordinary comings and goings.

People, ever envious of the rich and near-rich, noticed

when the owner of one of the big outfits rode in, expensively dressed and astride a horse most ordinary cowboys could only dream about but never afford. Stern-visaged, they strode with important purpose to the lawyer's office or the bank. Since cattle had replaced sheep in the hills outside of the town, most of the time the only Mexican the townfolk ever saw was a bull-whacker on a freight wagon or, even rarer, a die-hard sheepherder come for coffee or beans at the mercantile.

The two men who rode down the street on this warm, windless day were different. One was unmistakably a *vaquero,* a proud, hard-looking Mexican. Some noticed his horse—a fine, sturdy animal dancing with barely restrained power under the rider's perfect control. A lightly loaded packhorse followed on a short lead. A few eyes were drawn to the rider's fancy, silver-mounted saddle. All would later comment on the man's piercing dark eyes shaded by the big sugar-loaf sombrero.

Women not wishing to be seen parted curtains to study the young man dressed in tight-fitting black trousers flared over boots with plain working spurs, a short, embroidered jacket over his white shirt. The other man rode tall in his saddle. Older than the *vaquero,* he had the rawhide look of a Texan. His right hand loosely rested near the gun in his holster. Cold gray eyes scanned the street, doorways, alleys, and shadows.

The town's reputation was filthy in many ways. The devil made his home here, and Tilman, who knew that because he'd been here before, hoped to make this visit to Tascosa a short one.

The riders reined up at the sheriff's office and jail, where, as usual, a deputy sat out front in a ladder-back chair, plying his pocketknife and adding to a growing pile of wood shavings at his feet.

The *vaquero* spoke with the lawman, dismounted, dropped his reins over a hitching rail, then turned and motioned to Tilman. "He's in here." They followed the deputy inside.

"If a man has too much to drink and gets to raising Cain," the deputy explained, "we let him sleep it off here."

They passed from an outer office with a worn desk and chair, spittoon, gun rack, and stove to a block of cells in the back.

"He's in the middle cell. Door's not locked. You can take him out of here if you want to," the deputy said.

"Much obliged," the *vaquero* replied. Noonday heat was building outside, and not a breath of air came through the single small window in one wall. "Cam?"

"Who's that?" came a muttered answer from the cell.

"It's me, Juan Javier." The *vaquero* pushed his way into the cell, then recoiled at the smell of stale sweat and soiled bedding.

The man called Cam blinked, bloodshot eyes squinting at his unexpected visitor, then made a face and mumbled, "Ugh." He pulled a ragged quilt over his head. "Go get me a bottle, will you? I need some hair of the dog."

"Get up. Our mother sent me to bring you home."

"Always the obedient son," came the muffled, sneering reply. "Mama's favorite."

"Get up now!" Juan Javier said, jerking the straw tick mattress off the cot and spilling Cam onto the floor.

Cam came up swinging, a fist connecting with Juan Javier's jaw, staggering the bigger man with his surprise attack. Quickly recovering, Juan Javier drove a hard right into Cam's belly, followed by a straight left that caught Cam's brow and stunned him. Juan Javier then drove both fists hard into Cam's belly, taking his wind and collapsing the younger man into a heap. A boot dagger fell from Cam's hand and clattered across the floor. Juan Javier kicked the wicked blade under the cot. Fists cocked and ready, Juan Javier stood over the limp form of his younger brother, slowly relaxing when he saw that all the fight had gone out of Cam.

Tilman had his hand on his pistol, but he saw that Juan Javier could handle the problem. Tilman examined the wreck that sprawled on the ground. When he'd worked with the rangers, he'd seen men like this, and they always filled him with anger. Now he saw another side of the situation. Esperanza Stone's grief stood in the room with them. For the first time in his life, realization dawned on Tilman that for men like this one, there were mothers somewhere, maybe doing the same as Esperanza. It was different when you knew a person's family.

Months of a dissolute existence of drinking and gambling could not stand up against Juan Javier's hardened muscles, earned working outdoors day after day on the open range. Cam's looks—his black, wavy hair and his father's deep blue eyes—had probably kept him out of trouble when he was growing up and later proved a sure attraction for the women. However, the life he now led would soon turn him into another barroom nobody held together by whiskey and little else, Tilman reflected.

Juan Javier waited until Cam regained his senses and sat up on the floor. The smell of stale liquor and unwashed clothes filled the cramped cell. Cam rubbed the swelling on his brow where his brother's fist had landed. He finally saw Tilman. "Who's that? Another lawman out to get me?"

Juan Javier said, "This is Aunt Catherine's husband, Tilman Wagner. He and his family have come to help us."

"What is it with you, Juan Javier? You don't need help. I'm the one who needs help." Cam laughed at his attempt at a joke.

Juan Javier tried once again. "Cam, listen to me. For once think about something other than you and your needs. Our father's been hurt. He needs you. He needs both of us. Mother worries. Let's go home."

"Tell them I'll be home soon."

"They need you *now.*"

Silence.

"Cam, I beg you. We'll get you cleaned up, eat some breakfast, and be on the way home, where it's clean."

"Soon. I'll join you soon. I'm tired now. Let me sleep." Cam pulled himself onto the cot and turned from his brother to face the wall. "Leave me alone."

Disgusted, Juan Javier left the cell.

Cam's voice followed. "Hey, you got any money? I could use a few dollars."

"Leave him to rot." Juan Javier wouldn't look at Tilman as they started out of the jail. "I am ashamed he is my brother."

"Give me a minute," Tilman said. "You go get Cam's horse from the stables. I want to talk to the deputy. I promised your mother we'd bring Cam back, and I intend to do so."

Chapter Ten

At the sound of footsteps outside his cell, Cam, dozing on his jail cot, opened one bloodshot eye. "You again?" he muttered.

Tilman and Juan Javier swung the door open, and in the same way a man throws and ties a calf for branding, Juan Javier expertly slammed his brother to the cell's dirty floor and, using a rawhide piggin' string, immobilized his younger brother's hands and feet behind him. A protesting Cam writhed and contorted his body, shouting curses, much to the amusement of the deputy watching from the jail's office.

"Hush up," Tilman chided as he pulled Cam up by his shirt collar and rapped him behind the ear with a worn, leather-wrapped bag of lead shot. Cam went limp.

"Thanks," Tilman said, tossing the sap to the deputy.

"You bet."

A short time later the men rode out of Tascosa across the rough, broken scrublands of the Texas panhandle, a subdued Cam now tied to his saddle. At camp that evening, Cam begged to be released.

"I'll go peacefully," Cam complained. "You don't have to keep me tied up all the way home. You've cut off the circulation to my hands. I can't feel them, and they're all swollen."

"Can we trust him?" Tilman asked.

"I sure don't," Juan Javier scoffed.

"Well, we've got to let him go sometime. Might as well do it now."

Cam, overjoyed to be free of the biting rawhide, rubbed his hands and wrists and said, "I'll not try anything, I swear I won't."

Too tired to argue, Tilman and Juan Javier rolled into their blankets and soon were sound asleep.

Early the next morning, Tilman's fingers gingerly traced the edges of a huge, sore knot on his head. "At least it's not bleeding anymore."

"Tell me again how he did it," Juan Javier said.

"I always wake up before daybreak, and you both were still in your blankets. I was lighting a fire to make some coffee, and that's when he got me. I heard a sound, and I reckon he sneaked up behind me and used that chunk of wood there to whack me on the head."

"He's probably heading back to Tascosa. That place has some kind of hold on him. We'd better go get him again," Juan Javier said.

"No," Tilman said.

"What do you mean?"

"I mean, let him go. He's sold his soul for a bottle of whiskey and a deck of cards. If we bring him home, he'll only run off the first chance he gets, and if he doesn't run to Tascosa, it'll be some other place just like it. He's made up his mind, and we can't look after him all the time."

"But you told my mother you'd bring him home."

"I was wrong."

"So, what do we do?"

"We go back to the ranch and start over. We can handle this with Cam or without. We came for him because of your mother. Now let's go back to face Esperanza, and I'll take the blame for Cam's escape."

How had he let that boy get the goods on him and run off? Why had he been so willing to take Cam's word that he'd go along peacefully? Odd, when Juan Javier had told Cam that his father was hurt, the young man didn't even bother to ask if the old man was going to be all right. That boy needed to be taught a lesson.

Even so, it was not like Tilman to be fooled so easily. Was he getting too old for this?

The ride back to Lincoln County took several days, giving Juan Javier plenty of time to stew about his younger brother's lust for liquor, cards, and women. With Cam it was always about his own pleasure, with no thought of the consequences that he or anyone else might suffer. It galled Juan Javier that Cam could seem to do no wrong in his father's eyes. David Stone indulged his headstrong son with endless forgiveness and a constant supply of money to buy him out of trouble—money the family could hardly afford.

"You got something on your chest?" Tilman asked as they rode along late one morning. "You've been mighty quiet the last day or so. Spit it out."

"Why should I tell you my troubles?"

"I've been around. Maybe I can help. But for sure I can't help if I don't know the problem. So lay it out for me."

Juan Javier rode in silence.

Tilman gave up. He figured Juan Javier's pride would not let him talk, especially to someone he'd known for such a short time. It came as a complete surprise to Tilman when Juan Javier threw his head back and loosed a bloodcurdling cry at the skies above. Tilman's horse shied nervously.

"What is it?" Tilman asked.

"I am always picking up after Cam, and I feel that sometimes it is a hopeless task. It seems that I have spent my life being the good son. I wanted to continue school and learn about better ways to take care of our land and our stock. I wanted to know so much, but my father needed me at the hacienda when Cam disappeared. I am afraid the ranch is in danger of going broke unless we sell off most of the herds. And Cam's spendthrift ways meant that I had to give up any plans for improving the ranch's stock, since we have no money to pay for anything except the day-to-day necessities." Juan Javier released a torrent of words.

"After rustlers stole the summer herd, my father had to default on a beef contract, and there is no longer any money coming in," he continued, pouring out his frustrations. "Even though my mother has kept the books for the ranch and has tried to keep the creditors at bay, the merchants in Mesilla, Lincoln, Albuquerque, and Santa Fe are becoming more insistent that the bills be paid. The county sheriff, who collects taxes, will be coming soon too."

Once started, Juan Javier spilled all his pent-up anger about his brother. "How will we pay? Things are becoming desperate, and something has to be done. Yet my father still cannot say no to Cam. We could lose everything!"

Quietly Tilman rode with the young man, trying to think of the right words to reassure him. "I wish I knew all the answers to ease your mind."

"My mother said that you are family and that I can trust you."

"You can. What you say goes no further."

"*Bueno.*"

"All I do know is that Cam's your only brother. But nowhere does it say you have to like him or approve of what he does."

Chapter Eleven

The two men arrived back at the hacienda tired and exhausted. They rode across rangeland oddly devoid of cattle. Tilman studied his surroundings, looking, noting, a man accustomed to staying alive by his wits. Movement caught Tilman's eye—a running coyote, tongue lolling, paused to watch the riders pass before loping into the shadows. Juan Javier seemed lost in his thoughts, giving no indication that he even saw the creature.

"We'll ride up to the high meadow in the morning. See if we can find anything new." Juan Javier looked to Tilman, who nodded in agreement.

At the ranch, they found that David remained in bed, his wound healing slowly.

"Come with me for a moment, my son." Esperanza sensed the anger in her son and knew it had to do with Cam. "Tilman, if you will excuse us please?"

"Of course. Juan Javier, I'll see you tomorrow." He went to find Catherine, for he knew she'd want to know about Cam.

Esperanza and her trail-worn son sat in the parlor, quiet filled with words unspoken surrounding them. "Did you find Cam?" Before Juan Javier could answer, his mother reached for a pitcher and poured them some lemonade. Knowing her eldest, she waited for him to tell her what he had found in Tascosa.

"We tried to get him to come home, but he refused to listen to us." Juan Javier related their futile efforts. He left out the fact that they had found his brother in jail and that Cam had tried to use a knife on him. Neither did he say anything about having to use his fists to subdue his brother. She did not need to know how they had tied Cam and physically carried him from the town, only to lose him to the fierce draw Tascosa's fleshpots held for the young man. "The threat to the ranch means nothing to him. I didn't even tell him how badly Papá was wounded, because he can only see his own pleasure. Cam cares only for himself and wants what he can get in an easy way."

Esperanza knew that her eldest son was holding back some things to protect her feelings, but she could not bear to ask him to tell her more. Perhaps Tilman might tell her if she asked. It tore at her heart that her youngest son was drifting further away from the family, lost to his insatiable hunger for worldly pleasures. She lowered her eyes in momentary sadness and a growing shame she felt for failing to rear Cam to be a good man. Taking a breath, she gathered her strength. "*Bueno,*" she said. "Tomorrow you and Tilman will go and find out what is happening to our ranch."

"Yes," her son answered.

"Juan Javier, you are a good son. We are all proud of you. Don't ever forget that. I know what remaining here on this ranch has cost you. It is not all about Cam." She placed her cool hands on his brow in silent blessing and left him.

Chapter Twelve

The feeble light from a few kerosene lanterns on posts did little to push back the midnight darkness pressing down on the dusty streets of Tascosa. Here and there, yellow light spilled through the windows of saloons to fall onto plank boardwalks or, in the case of the more basic drinking palaces, onto the dusty gravel of the street. The Johnson House—a banner proclaimed its selection of fine tobaccos and imported wines and liquors—boasted double glass doors. Inside, a bald black man dressed in a white shirt with sleeve garters played the piano, entertaining himself with a lively tune he'd spent several days composing.

Two women waited in front of a highly polished bar that sported brass fixtures and foot rails, carefully nursing whiskey cocktails. Behind the bar were rows of liquor bottles with bright seals, an enormous mirror reflecting the bottles and the dull eyes that stood in sharp contrast to the painted faces of the two women. Oversized paintings hung on the walls—poor copies of Italian Renaissance works. Gaming tables took up most of the room.

The girls who worked the saloon floated through the haze and smoke, dispensing worn-out jokes followed by occasional whoops, masking their bone-deep weariness with false smiles. Most had not asked for this life, but life had dealt them this hand, and their only choice was to endure it until their looks faded, some drunk beat them up so badly that nobody would hire them, or disease overcame them and they ended up on the dark street corners. Rarely, a cowboy would offer marriage to some lucky girl, and, surprisingly, such unions often lasted, some even producing happy families.

The rooms upstairs belonged to a woman known as Rocking Chair Sue. Rumors abounded as to her original upbringing, but Sue kept her past a close secret. For tonight, at least, she belonged to Charlie Pickett, a man known in his own circle as a good judge of the many shades of weakness in men—and how to exploit them. Currently profiting as the small-time leader of a gang of cattle thieves, Pickett knew like the back of his hand this part of Texas and the meanness that ebbed and flowed through it. People didn't cross Charlie and get away with it. Sue put up with his offensive behavior because he kept others away from her and lavished good food and French champagne on her in exchange for her help stiffing the men who entered the bar with money in their pockets. There had been no romance in their arrangement for years. Only greed held them together.

In the shadows at one of the few tables still occupied, a table preferred by card sharps and professional gamblers, a long evening of poker seemed to be reaching a climax.

"These stakes are too rich for my blood." A gent in a tall hat turned his cards facedown.

"I'm out," a whiskey peddler grunted. "Seems luck is siding with you tonight, Pickett."

"I agree." A big-nosed man pushed his chair back as well. Noticing the look on Pickett's face, he quickly amended his speech. "Not that I'm implying anything . . ." He quickly stood, heading for the bar before he got in the way of Pickett's fists.

"Yeah, ya kinda have to wonder where all those cards came from," the peddler grumbled. "Mighty convenient, if I say so—"

With catlike suddenness one of Pickett's men pulled a leaded sap, and the peddler dropped facedown among the litter of cigarette and cigar butts, burned matches, spilled beer, whiskey, and dirt on the floor, never aware of what hit him. The bar tough dragged the limp figure to the door, threw him out into the night, and the game resumed. Pickett hated being challenged, and most who played with him learned that quickly.

Tobacco smoke hung low in the room, adding to the

smell of raw whiskey, burned kerosene from the lamps, and the sweet toilet-water scent of the tall woman named Sue across the table, standing hipshot by Charlie Pickett's side. Pickett's gaze above his cards was as cold and unblinking as a rattlesnake eyeing his next meal. The last of the men at the bar were calling it a night, staggering off to a bunk, a bedroll, or simply a wall to lean against to pass the night in a drunken stupor.

The piano player closed up, stretched, and went out the back as the barkeep blew out most of the lanterns, darkening the saloon.

"Five hundred dollars, Stone."

In a saloon where fifty dollars made for a high-stakes game, the few men still sober enough to understand what Pickett had said cast bleary eyes on more money being bet than they ever hoped to see in a lifetime. Cam Stone studied his cards. Once he'd gotten loose from Tilman Wagner and Juan Javier, he returned to Tascosa to take up business where he'd left off. For two weeks he'd done well playing the cards, but this deck had gone cold. His slide had started when he tried to draw to an ace high straight and got a deuce instead of a ten. Of the stacks of silver dollars, gold double eagles, two gold rings, and a down-on-his-luck Denver card slick's diamond stickpin he'd piled up earlier, everything he had was in the pot. He swallowed the knot in his throat. If he folded, he'd be broke. He'd discarded a five, hoping to get either a jack or a nine for "trips"—three of a kind. The ace he picked up did him no good. The two pairs he held would have to be enough.

"Will you help me out here?" Cam tried the sunny, boyish smile that always worked.

"Float you a loan?"

"I'm good for it. The RD will back me up."

"What outfit is that?"

"The Rocas Duras ranch."

"That's over in New Mexico Territory, ain't it?"

"Lincoln County. My family's ranch."

"Good enough for me. Go as much as you want." The smile didn't reach the man's eyes.

"All right. I'll see you and bump it another five."

Pickett tossed more money onto the table. "Pot's right. Let's see what you're so proud of, Stone." He spread his cards on the table. "Queens on tens. Can you beat a full house?"

Cam paled. "Not my night." He threw down his cards and stretched. "Reckon I'd best drift."

"Hold on, *amigo*."

Cam paused.

With a glance at Sue standing by his elbow, Pickett barked, "Gather up the pot for me." Turning to Cam, he said, "I'm a sporting man. You're good at cards, but luck wasn't on your side today. I hate to clean a man out, so why don't we have a friendly drink? I'll even give you a fair chance to win back some of your losses."

"My poke is pretty light. What do you have in mind?"

"I saw you racing some cowboys the other day. That's quite a horse you got. You think your mare can beat my nag?"

Cam said nothing. Back home he'd never lost a race riding China, his favorite mount. He'd seen Pickett ride in on a dish-faced roan that didn't look like much. This was definitely a chance to make good his losses.

"Your horse against that last pot—call it five thousand dollars. What do you say?"

Taking the man at his word, Cam jumped at the chance. With that much money he could make things right with his father. He gave no thought to the motive behind such generosity. "Done."

"Daylight tomorrow, down at the hay fields at the edge of town." An unseen nod passed between Pickett and Rocking Chair Sue as she hung on Cam's arm. Pickett slapped Cam's back. "Let's have that drink."

The drink became two. Then three. Cam hadn't realized how tall Sue was. Well, taller than he was, anyway.

"Cam, you are quite a man, are you not? The women probably adore you, don't they?" Sue looked into Cam's bloodshot eyes while she coyly twisted a lock of his hair in her fingers.

"I don't know, Miss Sue." Cam was drunk, and the woman's words filled his alcohol-soaked brain with delight. He wanted to impress her. "I guess I've had my share of women."

Caressing his arm, Sue poured him another drink. "This is from my special stock. Only for my favorite people."

"Where's Pickett?" Cam asked. "He said he was going to the outhouse, but he never came back."

Cam and the woman were sitting on an overstuffed red velvet love seat in a parlor. Parlor? When did they leave the saloon? The parlor light dimmed as the oil lanterns fluttered, and Cam ached with weariness. His head hurt, and he tried to remember what he had done earlier.

"Hey, sweetie. It's just you and me. Charlie must have called it a night." Sue had a taste for champagne, and she smiled at him as she refilled two fine crystal flutes. "Have another drink. I hate to drink bubbly alone."

Sue blurred and wobbled in Cam's vision. Cam smiled too. "Why not?"

At dawn the saloon's swamper shook Cam awake. He'd somehow ended up sleeping on a pool table. His mouth felt thick with a sour taste made worse by a pounding headache above his ears, and it hurt to focus his eyes. He threw up into a spittoon, wiped his mouth on his sleeve, and spat. Was Sue, her champagne, and the love seat only a dream?

Cam stepped onto the nearly deserted street in a useless attempt to compose himself. It was barely seven in the morning, and he was unshaven, had slept in his clothes, lost his hat somewhere, and had a monumentally nasty hangover. Had Sue slipped him something in the champagne? He ran a forefinger over his teeth in a crude attempt at cleaning them. It didn't work, so he wiped his finger on his pants. That wasn't the worst of his problems. He'd lost a lot of money, gotten suckered into a long shot at making up his losses, and he *still* owed Pickett all that money.

Then it came to him. He'd agreed to a race. At least that promised to be a breeze. He could do with a win. Luck had not been with him last night, and he hoped today would reverse his fortunes. Then maybe he could go home a winner, not broke.

An hour later Cam stood speechless in the early-morning light as a man he had never seen led China away. Cam turned to a smiling Charlie Pickett. "But I thought you'd ride that roan."

"That old crock? She's easy for gettin' around town but too old to run."

"You didn't tell me you had that Thoroughbred!"

"Boy, you didn't ask."

Cam's shoulders slumped in defeat. What would he do? Afoot and broke, Cam felt like he'd been played for the biggest fool in Texas. He should not have escaped from Juan Javier and that man, Wagner. He'd be almost home if he had stayed with them. Too late, he remembered what his father had told him: Never play the other man's game.

"Seems to me you're in way over your head, and your prospects ain't so good. First off, you need a job. Things ain't all that bad. You meet me at the Cattleman's directly, and we'll have a little breakfast and talk over your future." Pickett turned back to Cam. "You smell pretty bad and look even worse. Make sure you clean up a bit. Don't want to ruin my food."

Cam nodded, embarrassed and angry at the world. He didn't trust Pickett, but he had little choice. Not if he wanted to get back what he'd lost. But he'd have to be more careful in the future. He might be down, but he refused to stay that way. He was Carlos Abram Minear Stone, not a nobody. The odor of his body hit him as he staggered into his hotel room, and he nearly gagged. What was he doing with his life?

Chapter Thirteen

After an attempt at cleaning up, Cam started out for the Cattleman's Restaurant. Town gossip had it that men who crossed Charlie Pickett didn't live too long. Cam had two choices: try to run for it, or go through the door and face Pickett. He silently cursed Juan Javier and Tilman Wagner for allowing him to escape. This was all their fault. Why had they believed him, anyway? Now he was all alone.

Pickett had insisted he sign a marker for all that money, but so what? He'd slip away. It wouldn't be the first time. He'd done it down in El Paso del Norte a couple of years ago. Sure, his father had settled that debt for him when the man came looking for him. Then there was that time in Trinidad, when a faro dealer had cheated, Cam was sure, because nobody was *that* good. It wasn't *his* fault the cards were against him.

Why not run now? When things got bad, he'd always just skedaddled. After all, there were other towns, other women, other whiskey bottles. Besides, who'd know? Cam turned to walk away.

"Hey, you!"

"Sue?" Cam said as a perfumed hand closed over his arm and pulled him into an alley.

"Kid, Charlie's got a mean streak in him. He'll kill you before you reach the town limits," she said. "So you go in there and see what kind of deal he's got in mind."

"What if he kills me now?"

"If he does, at least you'll die facing him. Don't run with your tail tucked. Be a man, Cam. Get yourself in there and stand up on your hind legs and look him in the eye."

"What do you care?"

Her stare was cool. "Not now."

Did the hard, painted face soften, or was that just his imagination?

"Go on!" She pushed him toward the restaurant, yet still Cam resisted. "Look," she explained, "the barkeep knows your name. He told Charlie you've got a reputation for running out on a marker. His men are waiting, and if you try it, they know all the ways out of town. You won't get a mile before they find you."

Cam acknowledged the wisdom of Sue's words and headed for his meeting with Pickett. Soon, his mouth so dry he couldn't spit if he had to, he found himself sitting at a table across from Pickett.

"Coffee? You look like you could use some." Pickett raised a hand and beckoned the waitress. "Ham, eggs, fried potatoes, and biscuits for both of us, and keep that coffee coming," Pickett said to the girl. Turning to Cam, he said, "Don't worry. It's on me. We'll eat first, then talk."

"Sure. I could use a bite. Thanks."

By the time he'd finished eating, Cam felt somewhat better. At least he wouldn't die hungry, he thought. Pickett pulled a cigar from an inside coat pocket, bit the end off, spat, and fished around in another pocket for a match. "Smoke?"

"No," Cam answered. "Never picked up the habit." He relaxed a bit. " 'Bout the only habit I haven't acquired."

"Suit yourself," Pickett said. He leveled his eyes on Cam. "You're in pretty deep. The way I see it, you can welch and run, but do that, and I'll kill you. Bad precedent, you understand, if I let you go. Might encourage others to do the same, and then where would I be?"

"Don't much like that idea. Do I get another choice?"

Pickett studied the end of his cigar, the gray ash, the red glow, then the tightly rolled tobacco leaf. "You can make things right. One easy way is to get a letter off to your father. Tell him you got yourself into a heap of trouble, and you need a bank draft for five thousand dollars, right now, or you'll never see him again."

"But that's extortion!"

"Business, I call it. Anyhow, you should have thought before you made those bets, boy."

"What if my father won't pay?"

Pickett drew a forefinger across his throat in an unmistakable gesture. "You'd better hope he'll pay. Now, while you're waiting for him to bail you out, just to keep an eye on you, I'll put you on my payroll, and that way we'll not add any interest to your, uh, *loan.*"

"What kind of work would you have me do?"

Pickett waited until the waitress cleared the dishes off the table before continuing.

"Think about it. You're David Stone's youngest boy, over Lincoln County way."

"That's right." Rocking Chair Sue obviously knew her business. Pickett had the goods on him. Where was this leading?

"Chisum knows your folks. You all can come and go on his range anytime, and Chisum's boys don't bother you, ain't that right?"

"Yes, that's right," Cam said. "Why? What are you suggesting?"

"You and a couple of my boys are going to ride over to Chisum's range and push a few head of cattle back this way. I've got some buyers lined up who'll take fifty or sixty head at a time. If your dear father wants to see you alive, he'll move right quick on the draft. Won't take long to even things up between us."

"And if I don't join your rustlers?"

Pickett nodded toward a cold-eyed man sitting at a table across the dining room nursing a cup of coffee. "See him? He killed his first man when he was sixteen. I say the word, and he'll see to it you're planted six feet under by sundown." Pickett doused his cigar in Cam's coffee cup. "Then *I'll* write a letter to your daddy myself and explain to him about your debts and tell him I'm holding you until he stands good for it. He'll think you're still alive and pay up. So it don't matter none to me. You'll go along with it or else."

Cam hesitated. Sue had said to stand up to Pickett. But how? Pickett had him, and they both knew it.

"Look, boy." Pickett appeared to soften. "Don't you worry. Your family's rich, and a piddling five thousand won't make any difference to them. I ain't going to steal any stock from your pa. Chisum's got more cows than a dog's got fleas, and he won't hardly miss a few. Besides, he's sold out to some big cattle company from back in New York or England or someplace like that. He's just minding them steers until the company can sell 'em off." He laughed. "Chisum won't care if we make a few dollars off of them foreign stockholders!"

Cam stood. "Think I'll go clean up a bit and see if I can get me a horse, since mine is gone." He attempted to joke, knowing that his life was in the hands of the untrustworthy man at the table.

"Sure. Here, boy. Get a bath over at the hotel." Pickett made a big deal of fishing a couple of silver dollars from his coat pocket and tossing them onto the table. "And remember that old roan?"

Cam nodded as he pocketed the money. He couldn't afford to be proud.

"She's down at the stables. I've left word you're to pick her up." Pickett laughed. "Quite a trade."

Cam turned and left the restaurant, his ears burning as the laughter followed him down the street. He'd met old Chisum and didn't want to get involved, but he had dug a deep pit, and he couldn't climb out of it alone. He thought about wiring his father, but Juan Javier had told him things were tight, and Cam knew that he was the reason. There would be no letter, for there was no five thousand dollars lying around for his mistakes. Pickett would find that out soon enough. This time Cam had to handle things on his own. If he could.

Chapter Fourteen

"She's here, Mamá," Juan Javier called. Offering his left arm, he steadied his father, who had insisted on being out of his bed the past week and seemed determined to be up and walking, but carefully, with a cane. In front of the house the family gathered as Graciela Catherine Stone Baca and her husband, Santa Rosa Baca, descended from their shiny black phaeton with a dark red fringed top. The Spanish barb gelding pulling it was as black as night with red ribbon braided into its mane.

"How do you like it?" Graciela pointed proudly to the carriage. "Santa Rosa got it for me as a gift for presenting him with our Antonio." She beamed at her mother. "I am lucky, no?"

"That's a mighty fine horse and buggy you got there." Against Dr. Clark's orders, David was out of bed for short periods, after which he'd nap for hours.

"That's some animal, isn't it, Dad?" James admired the strong horse that stood in front of them.

Tilman agreed. He was taller than Rojo, younger, and probably a very valuable barb. "He reminds me of some of the racing Andalusians I've seen in Texas. They're fast." Tilman patted the horse's shoulder as he ran a hand along the animal's strong front legs. "I imagine this horse would give anyone a good race."

"David, when we get this settled, I hope I can talk you into selling Catherine and me a couple of these fine animals."

"Tilman, Catherine, James," Esperanza interrupted, "this is our daughter, Graciela, her husband, Santa Rosa Baca, and their new son, Antonio."

Tilman knew that Graciela's husband was an important banker in Socorro, but he would have guessed as much even had he not known. Santa Rosa's fine clothes and confident, easy manner bespoke a successful man well on his way to riches. They had made a special trip to meet Tilman and Catherine, and he appreciated the gesture.

"Graciela. Santa Rosa. The pleasure is mine." Catherine had slipped under Tilman's arm, and he liked the feeling of her right there beside him while James stood close by on the other side. His new family—how his life had changed! He'd been blessed with a second chance. Now he had not only a new wife and son but this extended family as well. Even in the midst of trouble there was hope. Life was good.

A quick glance at David's pale and sweating face

told Esperanza that her husband needed rest, so with open arms she shooed everybody into the house.

Tilman knew that Esperanza was planning a *baile*—a combination family reunion, homecoming, gathering, and dance—to introduce the Wagners and the newest addition to the family to their neighbors. Tilman hoped to have a chance to size up some of the folks from around the county, maybe discern who meant to harm David and his family. He hoped David would be up to it.

Santa Rosa joined the other men in the library. "Papá, do you think Cam will come?" he asked.

"I don't even know where he is." David shrugged.

"We know where he *was,*" Juan Javier said as he sank into one of the large chairs. "When Tilman and I found him in Tascosa a few weeks ago, we tried to bring him home. But he chose otherwise. He was in no condition to do us any good, anyway—is that not right, Tilman?" Juan Javier laughed, but the laugh was caustic. "However, we'll hear from him when he needs money again. Take my word for it."

"Don't talk about your brother like that," David said.

Stung by his father's public rebuke, Juan Javier answered, "I only speak the truth. You spoiled him, Father, with money and excuses, so why should we expect anything else?"

Tilman cleared his throat.

Santa Rosa went to the liquor cabinet and poured himself a glass of sherry.

Chapter Fifteen

"Beatriz! What are you doing? *Cuidado! Mija!* Be careful, and get down, now!"

"Aha! You must love me. You're speaking Spanish."

"Beatriz. If I have to come up there, I'll . . ."

"What? Oh!" Beatriz teetered on her precarious perch, then reached for a tree limb to steady the ladder while she strung a set of red, white, and green ribbons on the lower branches of the oak. "Isn't it pretty?" Smiling innocently at her mother, she gracefully descended and hugged Esperanza. "Do you not agree, Mamá?" Taking James by the hand, the two went into the house.

Graciela watched her sister. "It's always been this way with Beatriz. Thank goodness we were so different. I have always liked my privacy, but being with people brings joy to her and to them. How wonderful. But I could never be like her. I am too shy."

"Graciela, we'd never have had the patience for *two* like her." Esperanza shuddered at the thought, and the ladies chuckled quietly as they worked on completing the decorations. Company would be arriving soon, and much remained to be done. Small frosted cakes, sugared pecans, and other treats graced the long banquet table. The *cabrito*—goat—cooked on a spit near the house. Iron pots of rice and pinto beans simmered over the open fire pit, and a side of beef lay on a thick bed of coals, covered by a layer of coarse sand, slowly roasting since the day before.

"Any word from Cam, Mamá?" Graciela asked.

"No, Graciela. We have heard nothing from him."

"And are we surprised? When in the last three years have we ever known where our wonderful Cam, my illustrious brother, is?" Juan Javier stepped onto the gallery. His oldest son, playing with a stick horse, followed him.

"Juan Javier, that is enough. Today is a *fiesta* for our company. Behave, and no more of that talk." Esperanza reached for her young grandson, who hid behind his father's legs.

"Yes, Mother. I'll behave." Juan Javier dutifully gathered the remaining ribbons to place them in the trees. "I will finish hanging these. Our guests will be here in a short time."

Late afternoon brought southwesterly breezes across the open plains. It also brought the first of the neighbors from nearby ranches. The Stones rejoiced to see so many of their friends make time in their busy schedules to come celebrate. David, sporting a carved cane, wore tall black boots, a white shirt, and black pants. The bolo around his neck featured a large piece of silver-mounted turquoise. It reminded Tilman of the necklace he had brought Catherine from Santa Fe the year before.

Tilman looked at the people filling the courtyard. Did one or more of them want David's ranch badly enough to cause the trouble, even to try to kill David? He continued to study the crowd.

"She's over there, my brother." David nodded in the direction of the kitchen, and Tilman saw Esperanza and Catherine gracefully mingling with their guests.

Tonight, Esperanza appeared very patrician in a long, flowing red skirt with a black tapestry shawl featuring a red border interwoven with green, black, white, blue, and yellow. She wore it over a simple Spanish blouse, but even Tilman recognized the intricate design and knew that the shawl possessed a rich history.

Catherine looked very southwestern in a two-piece white cotton lawn dress. The pigeon-breasted blouse featured intricate lace and trim with tiny crochet-covered buttons closing the back. The full skirt also contained many lace insets that Tilman had watched her patiently piece together on their journey from Colorado. Catherine had wanted to look her best. She and Esperanza differed greatly in looks, one dark and the other fair, yet they complemented each other in all ways and were well on the way to becoming great friends.

"She's so beautiful," Tilman murmured of his wife.

"Whats that?" his brother-in-law asked.

Tilman laughed. "Did I speak out loud?"

"Newlyweds!" David chuckled.

"We are lucky, aren't we? God has blessed us all." The two men relaxed, neither one minding the silence between friends.

Tilman continued to watch the neighbors, looking for any hint of trouble or a clue as to who might be stirring up mischief. The young men surrounded Beatriz, and she clearly reveled in being the belle of the ball. Tonight, she was a vision in blue lace and taffeta, her matching fan tapping merrily from one hopeful young man's shoulder to another as she laughed and played the coquette. The fan had a language of its own, brash and challenging or shy, coy, a subtle movement sending perfume to this one or that one.

"My daughter is something, is she not?" David watched Beatriz. "Do you see the young man in the bright red shirt?"

A tall, blond, trim fellow chuckled at something Beatriz said.

"He is our neighbor's son, Walter Krell. He has been hopelessly infatuated with Beatriz practically since she could walk. Fortunately, he is a very patient man, or he would be tired of waiting for her by now."

"Do you and Esperanza like him?"

"He is a fine man and comes from a good family. Beatriz is still young, and we hope she eventually sees Walter for the man he will become." David paused. "However, right now she is in love with the world, so Walter will have to wait."

As they watched, a well-dressed rancher came up the drive in a shiny red one-horse runabout. Several men rode behind him. At a signal, the men continued to the bunkhouse a short distance from the main house. One of the riders, a shifty-eyed beanpole of a man, looked familiar to Tilman. The man saw Tilman watching and turned his face away, disappearing behind the bunkhouse.

A few minutes later the rancher made his way to his host and greeted David. "Mr. Stone. As a newcomer, I appreciate the invitation. Sorry to hear about your accident. Hope you're on the mend."

"Mr. Dunn. Glad you could come. Let me introduce you to my brother-in-law, Tilman Wagner. He and my sister are here visiting from Colorado."

"Pleased to make your acquaintance, sir." Cold blue eyes looked Tilman over, dismissing him at once as someone of no consequence. "Franklin Dunn at your service. I'm new to these parts myself." He continued. "I only recently arrived to take over the Wills place about a half day's ride from here. I'm still finding my way around."

Tilman nodded as he studied the man in front of him. Possibly in his midforties, his clothing indicated wealth, but something about his manner did not. No, this man was of the newly rich. He wore—no, he *flaunted*—his wealth for all to see. Something about the man urged caution.

"Where did you say you were from, Mr. Dunn?"

"Here and there. I've been all over and finally decided it was time to settle in one place and start a family." His gaze centered on the group in the courtyard, especially on Beatriz, and the open hunger on Dunn's face told Tilman whom he had in mind for a fitting wife.

"Mr. Dunn buys cattle for some packers in the northern states and has several other irons in the fire." Talk of cattle superseded the earlier conversation as a few of the ranchers joined the men, and Tilman stood listening to the conversation while watching Franklin Dunn. Something didn't sit right, and Tilman remained wary of the man's glib manner.

Within the hour, the sun became fiery red as it slowly disappeared behind the distant hills. Chinese lanterns glowed, and groans could be heard from those who had eaten too much. A mariachi band, playing a type of music popular among the descendents of the original Spanish settlers of Mexico, began to serenade the guests. The sky above clear and blue, the evening cool and comfortable, it was a night made for dancing.

Esperanza and Juan Javier led the couples on the dance floor, for David still needed his cane and would not be dancing for weeks to come. Tilman and Catherine took the floor. The music had a life of its own and beckoned the watchers from their seats. Beatriz and Walter whirled by, deep in conversation, only to be interrupted by Franklin Dunn. As the older man and Beatriz promenaded around the floor, Walter clearly struggled to control his temper. His father approached his side and said something, and the two men disappeared into the dark.

"That is not a happy young man," Catherine whispered into Tilman's ear. "Who is the older gentleman monopolizing Beatriz?"

Tilman quickly explained about Franklin Dunn. "I keep thinking I recognized one of his riders when they arrived, but I can't place from where."

"Do you think from when you were in Texas?"

"I don't know, Mrs. Wagner." Tilman held Catherine a little closer. "But I do know that that Mr. Dunn bears watching. He wants a wife, and I'd bet my last dollar he's set his sights on Beatriz."

"But, Tilman, she must be half his age."

"Not that uncommon around here. You have to admit she is a beauty, smart and from a good family with land." Tilman guided Catherine around the courtyard, the music changing to a lively beat, and all attempts at conversation stopped.

James danced awkwardly by with one of the young girls. Clearly he had no idea what he was doing, treading on his partner's feet, his lips moving as he counted his steps, but he was apparently having a wonderful time. Tilman and Catherine watched their shy son in astonishment. It was a magical night indeed.

Chapter Sixteen

Worn out from dancing, Catherine sought momentary refuge in the kitchen to see if Esperanza needed help. Tilman also needed to take a break. The far *pórtico* offered quiet and a breath of cool, fresh air, but he found himself overhearing a private conversation.

Separated from the crowd and musicians, heated words between Juan Javier and David were clear in the relative quiet. From what Juan Javier said, Cam had taken some money when he ran off this last time, and now David was having trouble paying his debts because of that. Tilman, realizing that this conversation was but a new rendition of what must be an old song between David and Juan Javier, cleared his throat to make his presence known. Then he moved from the shadows to join three ranchers who'd come out for a smoke.

David and his son left the *pórtico* to go inside the house, the conversation clearly not over.

"Are the rustlers around here hitting you hard?" Tilman asked the ranchers.

The two younger men deferred to a trim, silver-haired, older man named Tijerina. "They become bolder each day. The cancer that grows in La Placita—you call it Lincoln—spreads even up here in the foothills below Sierra Blanca. The rustlers form gangs with fearful names. Some call themselves Los Diablos, others the Soldiers Ring, and there is even one called the Church Ring."

" 'Ring'?" Tilman asked.

"That's right. Some specialize in stealing horses, others cattle. They ally themselves with factions in Santa Fe. They ride with impunity, for it is said that they have the protection of friends in the Santa Fe Ring, men in the Territorial government."

"Why do you call it a 'ring'?"

"When one tries to find the head of the snake to cut it off, one finds an endless circle of clues that lead nowhere and to no one—like walking around a ring that leads one back to the beginning. There are men from across the Texas border, in Tascosa, led by a man named Pickett. They have caused some trouble close to here."

Tilman paused. Pickett? Had Cam said something about playing cards with a Pickett? He needed to find out.

"We thought the Lincoln County War was finished

last year, and things were getting better since the troubles were over. Then Stone lost his entire herd to rustlers. Stolen," the one called Hartman said.

"How many were in that herd?"

"More than eight hundred, I believe. A mixed herd of steers and cows," Hartman said. "Not the runty cattle most of us raise around here, with no meat and backbones like knives—little bitty things. Stone had put together some good stuff, most at least half-blood Herefords. That Juan Javier has a good head for breeding cattle. He's mixing Herefords and Durhams to get the most meat. He's pretty good with horses too, as I believe you have seen."

"But what about the drovers? What happened to them?"

"Two were killed. The others have not been seen."

"The cattle have likely been rebranded by now and sold off to contractors at prices none of us could tolerate," the other man allowed. Grinding his cigar into the ashtray on a table, he demonstrated his regard for such contractors. "We suspect we know some of the agents working for the beef contractors who deal with the rings."

"Let me see if I get your drift," Tilman said, trying to make sense of the ominous tale he was hearing. "This problem is not just a once-in-a-while thing but ongoing. Correct me if I'm wrong. I'm trying to work through this. I knew that Lincoln County was having trouble, but I didn't realize the rustling came out here. Sounds to me that if some of these so-called contractors don't arrange to steal cattle themselves, they have their agents buy them from the rustlers."

"That's correct," Tijerina said. "We understand the rustlers deliver stolen cattle at five dollars a head, while we cannot afford to sell the same class of cattle for less than fifteen dollars. With rustled cattle, a dishonest contractor might make good money even at two dollars a head."

"Rustling ain't all of it. There's been some hay fields burned too," Hartman said. "Drift fences have been cut, and a couple of fellows that live a-ways out are gone. Vanished, I mean. Nobody's seen or heard tell of them."

"That's right," Tijerina said. "And when their ranches are sold for debts, always the same lawyer comes to buy them."

"Any idea who he represents?"

"No one knows. Someone uses that lawyer and leases some of the fenced range for his stock," Hartman said. "The boys say that the grass over there must be better than the grama our cows feed on, because that stock breeds faster than anybody ever saw."

Tijerina cleared his throat, and as if on signal the three excused themselves to find their wives. The men could not conceal their worries about the increasing lawlessness in the area. However, since Tilman was not known to them, they clearly feared they might have said too much. Tilman puzzled over all he'd heard.

"Wagner!" A voice came from the deeper shadows in the yard bordering the *pórtico.*

Tilman turned to look, squinting into the darkness. "Who's that?"

A figure moved into the dim light, and when Tilman saw the face of the man who confronted him, his hand involuntarily reached for a gun—but he was unarmed.

"I ain't heeled neither," the skinny man said, raising his hands at waist level to show he had neither gun belt nor a pistol stuck in his waistband.

"Fields," Tilman said. "I thought I recognized you slipping into the bunkhouse earlier tonight."

"It ain't 'Fields' around here." The man swore an oath, coughed, and spoke again. "Wagner, I done three years in Huntsville Penitentiary on account of you."

"As I recall, you were sentenced to ten years. You hurt that woman pretty bad. I don't reckon you got out early on good behavior."

"She was just some wore-out saloon girl," the man said. He coughed several times, then struggled to catch his breath. "Nobody cared."

"You were wrong. The law cared," Tilman said. "So what happened?"

"I run off from a work gang a-pickin' cotton on some judge's farm. Got tired of makin' his crop for no pay. Wagner, I swore I'd get even with you for puttin' me there." Another cough. "You remember that?"

"You figure this is the time?"

"Naw. I'm gonna enjoy this, with you wonderin'

what I'm up to and all. Say, I noticed a mighty pretty lady with you. Is she your wife? She'd make a good-lookin' widow for some lucky man."

"You, for instance?" Tilman sneered. "You won't live that long."

"I ain't the marryin' kind. I just love 'em up real good and leave 'em."

Tilman's anger flared at the man's reference to Catherine. "Fields—or whatever your name is now—I'll not stand for your threats. I'm not the law anymore, and I've got other things on my plate, but you'd best remember that you're a fugitive escaped from prison. Next time I see you, you be armed, or I'll kill you on sight."

"Keep a-lookin' over your own shoulder, Wagner. The time you don't is the time I'll be there." The man slipped away into the darkness as Catherine came through the door.

"There you are." Catherine appeared by his side. "Who was that you were talking to?"

"Oh, nobody you'd know."

"There are lots of people here I don't know," she said. "Try me."

At Tilman's silence, Catherine prodded. "What I heard you say just now was the kind of thing you used to say when you first came to Colorado, looking for Dan's killer. But you've changed, haven't you?"

"I will never allow anyone to talk about you the way that man did."

Catherine placed a hand on his arm. "Words, Tilman—that's all they were."

"Well . . ." Tilman wanted to divert Catherine from the moment. He didn't want to frighten her. "I think I've learned what caused David to send that telegram asking for help. The first problem is the rustlers. But there's more to it."

"Are you going to tell me about it?" Catherine leaned closer to her husband, safe in his arms. God had truly blessed her with this man.

"Well, Juan Javier is a bright and ambitious man with a good feel for stock, and David relies on him to be here. He should, on account of he's the older of the two sons. That younger one, Cam, from what I gather, loves the women and has a weakness for cards and strong drink. Not a good combination."

"Go on," Catherine said.

"There're hard feelings between Juan Javier and Cam, and between Juan Javier and David. Cam has about cleaned out David's ready cash, and since he lost the cattle and horses, David's prospects are not looking good."

"Esperanza told me this is the only Spanish grant in Lincoln County. She said Santa Rosa Baca has a copy of all the legal documents locked away in his bank. But she worries that they'll lose everything," Catherine said. "What can we do?"

"We'll help in any way we can, but we have to know more about the men behind the troubles."

Esperanza swept onto the porch. "There you are. I am a poor hostess that my guests of honor are left alone out here!" She glanced at the two as they stood in the candlelight. "You two newlyweds look younger than Graciela and Santa Rosa. You also look too serious for such a beautiful evening. Come and let me introduce you to a few more of our neighbors."

Chapter Seventeen

The full moon and the stars reflected on the surfaces of the dark wine in crystal glasses around the table. The night was almost as bright as day. Whenever Esperanza looked, Franklin Dunn was cutting in to dance with Beatriz. As the evening progressed, Dunn became bolder and bolder, cutting in on nearly every dance. Many of the young men gave up and went to find other young women, but Walter Krell matched him dance for dance, cutting in on Dunn. The tension between the two men grew, and Esperanza looked for David. She didn't want a scene. The Krells were good neighbors, and Walter's mother, Hilde, was a special friend.

"Are you looking for David, Esperanza?" Catherine stood beside her. "Tilman helped him inside to rest for a few minutes. The excitement was too much for him. After a short rest he'll be back out." Catherine's gaze followed her sister-in-law's. Beatriz and Franklin Dunn waltzed around the courtyard.

Mesmerized by the smoothly charming older man, Beatriz laughed, tapping her fan on Franklin's shoulder in mock reprimand. She batted her eyes, enjoying his admiring gaze. Esperanza wasn't sure what to do. Franklin Dunn fascinated Beatriz. A dangerous situation, for sure.

Esperanza approached Beatriz, only to be intercepted by one of her departing guests. Suddenly the music stuttered and died away. She turned to see a tableau in the flickering light of the strings of bobbing Chinese lanterns. Beatriz stood between Franklin Dunn and Walter Krell. The two men loomed over the young woman, unblinking, waiting to see who would make the first move.

"Mr. Dunn, I think you must be getting tired of all this dancing. A man your age should take care," Walter, his face flushed and his hands in fists by his side, goaded the older man. "Maybe you should rest a while and catch your breath, while we younger fellows dance with Miss Beatriz."

"I don't think that's necessary, boy. Apparently Miss Beatriz prefers a man of the world over a young pup like you."

Beatriz moved to break the tension. "Please, gentlemen. The night is late." The remaining people in the courtyard watched quietly, many of the younger men nodding agreement with Walter. She spoke above the low murmur of voices from the guests. "My father does not need trouble here as well."

"Your father and your brother seem to be with Mr. Wagner someplace else." Franklin looked around. "I haven't seen them in quite a while."

"Which is why you have tried to monopolize Beatriz. You are twice her age," Walter challenged, "so why don't you and I discuss this outside by the barn?"

"Gentlemen. Beatriz." Esperanza took Dunn's arm. "I believe that you and I haven't danced tonight. Perhaps we might show these youngsters a thing or two, no?" Esperanza turned to her daughter. "Beatriz, some of our guests are leaving. Will you go and see if you can help them get their things while Señor Dunn and I take the floor?"

Esperanza had smoothly compared Dunn's age to hers. The music started up again, but Dunn brushed her hand from his arm rudely. Beatriz stood still, barely breathing. Walter remained at her side, silent but watchful.

"No, Mrs. Stone. I think I am danced out for the evening."

Esperanza gently pushed Beatriz with her hand. "Beatriz, *por favor*. See to our guests, *mija*."

"Walter?" Catherine slipped quietly in front of Walter and took one of his clenched fists in her hand. "Could you help me find your mother's dishes, please?" She ushered him toward the kitchen. "The food was excellent, and we have a pile of dishes to be sorted." She nodded to Franklin. "Mr. Dunn, please excuse us."

Neatly outfoxed by the two women, Dunn had no choice but to bow gracefully and leave the floor. His time would come.

The other dancers returned to the floor. The young men, realizing there would be no fight, rushed to find partners for the last dances of the evening. Franklin Dunn looked at no one as he departed to find his buggy. Esperanza was afraid that her family had not seen the last of Mr. Dunn's anger.

Before he climbed into the little runabout, Dunn called his men together and instructed the man called Fields that he had no need of them until the next day.

"Mount up, boys, we're heading for town! The first round's on the boss." Quickly the cowboys howled into the darkness, their excited shouts turning heads as Tilman stepped into the courtyard.

Chapter Eighteen

The guests staying overnight retired for the evening as the night gave way to early morning. Many of the neighbors who lived any distance from the RD had set up tents on the grounds, and small campfires flickered in the moonlight.

In the Territory, great distances often separated ranches, and such parties represented both a social treat as well as a challenge. Neighbors often traveled several days and thus planned to stay at least a day or two in order to visit and catch up on news and see friends and family. Those who lived closest headed for their buggies for the ride home, intending to return the next day. Living on remote ranches meant weeks and months of little company, no news or gossip, and so when anybody threw a party, it was thoroughly enjoyed by all.

Tilman sat alone at a small table in the coolness of

the courtyard, a pitcher of *sangria* and several glasses untouched before him. Dunn's laughing and shouting men were out of sight and hearing, the dust of their leaving settling in the light air of a now peaceful evening. Multicolored Chinese lanterns bobbed gently in the breeze, creating moving shadows on the courtyard walls. David came from outside and closed the gate.

"Mind if I join you?"

"Please do," Tilman answered.

David poured a glass of *sangria,* then nodded an unspoken question at Tilman, who declined. David eased himself into the chair opposite Tilman, pain from his recent wound showing on his face. "I'm sorry you had to hear that tonight."

"A man's going to have troubles with his son."

"Both of them, in my case."

"I think that's the way for all men. Your boy fights you, and then one day you realize that he isn't a boy any longer, and he can whip you if he wants." Tilman looked at the early-morning sky, the faint gold of the sun's rays, almost ready to push back the night. "David, you're so worried about Cam, you can't see what's going on around you."

"What do you mean?"

"Somebody's already tried to kill you. Stealing your cattle, killing your drovers, and running off your horse herd is bad, but I'm betting there's more to it than that, and it could get worse. Why, look what happened to Esperanza the day we arrived."

"Explain yourself."

"Think about this. Why isn't the open range enough for running cattle? There's plenty of land to be had around here, and it's cheap enough for any man willing to work for it. But the difference between open range and your spread comes down to one simple fact. You've got water on your land, and the man who controls that much water controls most of this range, all the way to the Pecos River."

"This land is ours. It came down from Esperanza's grandfather, who got the original grant, to her father, and since he had no surviving male heirs, in the way of the old Spaniards it went to her. Mateo, Esperanza's father, changed his will to include me as well before he died, as he foresaw the problems this rich piece of land could cause when the *Anglos* started arriving in this area."

David continued. "This way the land is in the hands of both nationalities. Mateo was a very clever man. The land is all properly surveyed, confirmed, and deeded at Santa Fe. If I die, Juan Javier and Cam get the ranch and in turn see that Graciela and Beatriz are taken care of as well."

"I've heard talk about the grant and how it came to you, but I don't understand it," Tilman said. "Explain it to me, so I'll know what we're facing."

"It's like this. In 1848, when the Mexican War ended, the United States got Nuevo Mexico and a whole lot of other territory under what they call the Treaty of Guadalupe Hidalgo. One of the articles of that treaty said in so many words that for Mexicans around here owning property, it was still theirs, and the Americans would not take it away. Then, a few years later, the Federal government set up a Surveyor General of New Mexico Territory to look into land claims under the laws of Spain and Mexico. He confirmed the validity of our grant, the one we call the RD, to the United States Congress. That's all on file in Santa Fe, and a copy of everything is in a bank vault in Socorro."

"Seems your title is legal enough," Tilman said. "But there's more, isn't there?"

"There is. Back in 1879, two things came together. Folks got land greedy, because the railroads reached Las Vegas, opening eastern markets for our produce, and the Territorial government saw a chance for more revenue, so they passed a property tax law. It turned out to be another way to skin a lot of poor and illiterate *Hispanos* out of their land. We had the money to pay taxes, but a lot of good folks around here saw their lives put up on the block to be sold at sheriffs' auctions."

"What kind of shape are you in now? For taxes, I mean, now that your herd's been stolen and cash money from a sale won't be coming in. A place this big must take a lot to operate."

David's face paled. The hand holding the wineglass trembled briefly but then stopped. "It was the Banditti, one of the gangs, who stole my cattle and my horses. They took the stock for easy money with no work. They don't want the land. My sons will know how to help me keep the RD going."

"Maybe someone else wants this land badly enough that he's willing to kill to get it. Juan Javier has a good head on his shoulders and knows horses and cattle. But my question is, do you have the cash?"

"Esperanza keeps the books for us. She does not say she is worried."

"All right. Have you thought about the fact that Cam might already be dead? How long since you heard from him?"

"Cam's run off before. He goes off gambling, womanizing, and when he gets his fill, he comes back with his tail between his legs."

"Are you making good on his gambling debts?"

"I'd rather we talked about something else."

"Cam's going through your cash money, and rustlers have seen to it that you don't have any coming in. I hope you have a pile of gold stashed away in a poke buried out back. But answer me this: If you've got enough stashed away to see you through this, why did you send that telegram?"

"I didn't. Esperanza did. You know how women are. They see ghosts in the night. She's high-strung, and she acted without thinking."

"Harrumpf," Tilman grunted. As far as he could tell, Esperanza seemed remarkably levelheaded. Why had David implied otherwise?

"Anyway, I talked to Dunn tonight," David said. "He represents a Chicago meatpacker, and we've agreed on a beef contract guaranteeing a higher price per head than most ranchers are getting. All have to do now is round up the cattle we missed on the last drive and get them to the railroad at Las Vegas. We can probably find five hundred out there, even if we do have to mix some old cows with the young stuff."

"You're talking about your breeding stock."

David paused. "Yes."

"I don't know, David. This is your place, your family, and your future. But sometimes a stranger sees what one familiar with things might miss. I don't want to interfere, but there's something about Franklin Dunn I find not quite straight. I'm not sure I understand what it is, but there's a coldness to him that I find mighty disturbing. I'd be very careful where he's concerned. Plus there's his interest in Beatriz."

David smiled. "All the men find Beatriz attractive. That is a curse and a blessing for Esperanza and myself. It means nothing."

"If you'd seen Dunn and young Walter earlier this evening, you might be more concerned. 'Nothing' is not how I'd describe their encounter. Esperanza and Catherine defused the situation before I could do anything. But 'nothing'?"

"I know you mean well, Tilman, and I respect the fact that you're used to this kind of thing, but maybe, like Esperanza, you're seeing dangers lurking in the shadows where there are none. On big ranches, things happen. We've just had a string of bad luck. It'll be all right."

David used his cane to pull himself up, the strain of the evening showing on his tired face. "I think I'll go rest for a while. The neighbors will be showing up for something to eat in a few hours." He looked over the field, noting the small fires and tents visible through the large patio gates. "Reminds me of the war, when we camped out." He smiled with sadness and limped into the house.

A restless and uneasy Tilman found Catherine tucking James into bed for the night. "The moon's full, and it's plenty light out, so I'm going to saddle up and go for a ride."

"At this hour?" Catherine asked.

"I've got some thinking to do," he answered, taking his gun belt down from a hook in the wardrobe and buckling it on. "Just a precaution, Catherine. There are still wolves in these hills." The two-legged kind, he meant, more vicious than any pack of *lobos* that ever stalked an elk.

Chapter Nineteen

Esperanza found Tilman leaving the house, wearing a gun, but said nothing about it. When she asked why he was riding out, he told her of his concern about Dunn and Fields. "Be careful," she urged.

Tilman slowed his horse to a walk when he spotted the scattered lights of the old but troubled Spanish settlement of La Placita, partly masked by tall cottonwood trees. A confrontation with Fields was possible, but even so, what better place to go and ask questions? Saloons where men gathered to socialize over a few drinks were always good sources of information about local goings-on. Besides, Fields had to be dealt with, so why not now? No man could threaten Catherine, not while Tilman drew breath.

Darkened, false-fronted buildings, a few homes, some wood-framed and some of adobe construction, lined the single street through the town. Yellow light from lanterns and the sound of men's voices poured from the windows and front door of an adobe saloon. Several horses stood by a hitching rail, where Tilman tied his mount. A few men turned to see who had come in, but since the tall man was a stranger, he elicited little notice. Drinking and loud talking continued as Tilman elbowed his way into an empty space at the bar.

"Rye," Tilman said to the barkeep, "and one for yourself."

"Thanks. Don't mind if I do," the man answered.

"How about a champagne flip for me?" a woman said, placing a hand on Tilman's arm.

"Some other time." Tilman shook his head after glancing at the skimpily dressed woman.

"Beat it, Lou," the barkeep growled.

"Aw, c'mon, Dave," she complained. "Pickett run me off so's I won't hear him and the boys talk about some big job they're gonna pull off. If nobody'll buy me a drink and dance with me, how'm I supposed to feed my young'uns?"

"Call it a night, Lou." To Tilman he said, "Pot of stew on the stove if you're hungry."

"No thanks." Lou's whining was attracting unwanted interest from down the bar, and Tilman didn't want that. Tucking a five-dollar gold piece into Lou's bodice, Tilman said, "For your kids."

"Thanks, mister." The woman scurried for the door. The five dollars probably represented a week's earnings for her.

"Say," Tilman said to the barkeep, "know of any jobs around here?"

"Friend, punching cattle draws gun wages in these parts. No offense, but you don't have the look of a man needing that kind of work."

"None taken. Say, who's the bull of the woods around here?"

"You're fishing. Just who is it you want?"

Tilman raised the glass to his lips. "Dunn."

"Yeah? Look around you. These are his boys."

"He on the up-and-up?"

"Mister," he snorted, "you name it, and he's in it. Don't say I told you, but . . ."

Before he could say more, a raucous cry from down the bar demanded another bottle. Some of the boys were just short of blind drunk already. They'd drink as long as they had money in their pockets and be thirsty until next payday.

"I seen you," a slurring voice came from behind Tilman. "Over at Stone's place."

A look in the mirror behind the bar showed a slouching, hard-eyed young cowboy, empty beer schooner in one hand, glaring over Tilman's shoulder. Tilman turned to face the man.

"Hey!" the man shouted, dropping the schooner and fumbling aside his vest with his right hand, reaching for the gun in his waistband, tugging hard. But the pistol's front sight blade caught in his pants. "Here's that fellow Fields was talking about." He looked down in exasperation at the weapon he couldn't draw.

Tilman stayed the man's hand with his own right while stepping in to throw a straight left to the man's jaw, snapping his head back and sending his hat flying. The cowboy sagged to the hard-packed dirt floor. Tilman quickly drew his own gun and barked to the men in the room, "Don't anybody go for it! You'll be dead before you clear leather."

"Easy, boys," the bartender said, leveling a sawed-off shotgun across the bar at the men in the room, the sound of the hammers being cocked loud in the sudden silence. "No gunplay in here. The sheriff is in the back room, and there'll be hell to pay if you interrupt him."

All eyes remained on Tilman, but nobody wanted to challenge that shotgun.

"You owe me for the drinks, friend," the barkeep said to Tilman. "Then you'd best be on your way."

As Tilman tossed a couple of silver dollars onto the bar, his gaze found Fields. The man was passed out under a gaming table at the other end of the bar, his breath wheezing. Tilman's eyes narrowed as he swung his gun to bear on Fields.

"Uh-uh," the barkeep said, motioning toward the door with the shotgun.

"Yep." Tilman nodded. "You're right. Thanks, friend."

Outside, Tilman untied the horses at the rail and slapped one, spooked the others, and with a shout and wave of his hat sent them running into the darkness. He mounted up and spurred his horse into a run. Behind him came angry shouts and guns flashed in the night as drunken men blasted several shots in his direction.

Tilman followed the road back toward the RD. Would he have shot Fields? He had no ready answer. If it came to that, he'd rather be looking the man in the eye when he drew trigger. But what would Catherine think of him?

Chapter Twenty

Three days after the *baile* at the Stones' ranch, Franklin Dunn sat in El Oso Grande, an open-air cantina in Santa Fe. He disliked the dusty adobe city with its noisy, crowded, narrow streets and alleys. A capitol, even if it was only a territorial capitol, ought to be different. The seat of a government should look like the engravings of ancient Rome he'd seen in a book, or like Constitution Avenue in Washington. Dunn would do what he had to and then leave.

Arriving the previous night, he was ready to set the stage for dealing with the Stone family. They were a problem. Dunn wanted their ranch, the Rocas Duras. When it became his, he would have completed the final step to becoming the cattle baron he imagined himself to be, a power in the Territory. With Beatriz Stone at his side, his empire secure, Dunn would be his own boss, and nobody else could tell him what to do. Important men would seek him out for his advice and counsel. Careful planning had led to this moment, and Dunn savored the thought. He pulled out his pocket watch and checked the time. Fifteen minutes.

"*Señor.* Would you like a drink?"

"Tequila."

"Excuse me. Mr. Dunn?" A timid-looking man wearing a faded, threadbare suit stood by his table, hands nervously worrying an equally faded bowler hat. Thin strands of hair were combed from above his left ear across his balding pate to the other ear. Even the gentlest breeze lifted the strands, so the little man frequently reached up to pat them back into place. Dunn tried not to look.

"Mr. Means, I take it?" Dunn impatiently motioned for the mouse of a man to sit.

Means twisted his hands together as he looked around, agitated, as if frightened of something. "Are you sure this is the place we should meet? What if we're seen?"

"Don't worry about it, Mr. Means. Sometimes out in the open is the best place to do private business." Silently he thought that, of all people, this man was the most offensive type, one afraid of his own shadow. Dunn hated dealing with weak men. You couldn't trust them. Nevertheless, Dunn's plan required that he take a man like this one into his confidence. He'd learned at an early age that getting ahead sometimes demanded the sacrifice of his principles to get what he wanted. He pulled out a chair and pointed. "Sit, man."

Mr. Means sat, ordering a cup to tea and fanning himself with a paper. "It is so hot out here."

"Well, if you can help me, then you can go back east or to Europe or wherever you want."

"I, n-n-n . . . Yes, I can," Mr. Means stuttered, his hands clenched while he explained. "I've worked in this job for t-t-ten years and am no better off than before." His confidence returned. "I need a new start, and I'm tired of waiting. That's why I'm here."

Dunn waited to hear what else Means had to say. At least the man was showing a modicum of gumption.

"I located the papers you asked about." Means nervously broke the silence. "I had to hunt, but I found them, and, unfortunately, they are in good order. The original title to the Rocas Duras ranch is a Spanish grant made to Mrs. Stone's ancestors in the 1700s. Before Mrs. Stone's father, Mateo Javier de la Garza, died, he had the title to his lands legally transferred to his daughter and her husband, David Stone. This happened nearly fifteen years ago." He paused. "I give him credit. He knew it would be only a matter of time before someone would want to take that land. It holds too much promise." Means paused. "He had the land confirmed by the Territorial government and recorded, so the new laws would not circumvent his claim."

"So, how do we break the title?"

"We can't. Clear title is recorded in the courts for New

Mexico Territory, and it has been done by a lawyer who knows his business."

"Well, fix it, man!" Franklin spat, "I'm not paying you to tell me it's unbreakable!" He tried to control his temper as men at nearby tables turned to look his way.

"It will cost quite a bit more than we had agreed on, I'm afraid. Accidents are costly." Mr. Means held his breath, seemingly amazed at his own temerity. "If papers are lost or destroyed, though, then who can prove they were ever there?" He sat back in his chair, waiting.

"Very well. I'll double the money. What I already gave you, I'll double on the other end, but I want you out of Santa Fe before anything gets out. Then I'll have your money sent to Albuquerque, and we'll both be in the clear."

The two men shook on the deal, made final plans, and Mr. Means left. He had a lot to do and a short time to do it.

Chapter Twenty-one

In his hotel room the following evening, Dunn awakened from a deep sleep to bugle calls and a hubbub of shouting men. Pulling a bathrobe over his nightshirt, he flung open the window and leaned out. Smoke. Often Santa Fe smelled of the smoke from thousands of cooking fires, usually burning piñon pine and scrub juniper common to the region. Their aroma added to the sharp smell of "town" gas extracted from coal to supply the city's modern streetlights, but this was different, acrid. The old saying, "Where there's smoke, there's fire," came to Dunn's sleep-fogged mind. His eyes burned, and he wrinkled his nose when the night breeze brought the odor of burning wood. He imagined he smelled burning paper and glue. He wanted to believe the smell was real.

Down the street, smoke billowed from the basement

windows of the Federal Land Office building. A fire company was on the scene, and in the street several uniformed men snaked hoses from a horse-drawn reel cart near a water tanker. Others unhitched two big Belgian horses from a brightly polished Silsby steam fire-engine that belched a spark-lit cloud of black smoke as pressure built in the pumps. Well-trained firemen quickly made connections tight. The engineer's hands danced across valves and wheels, and a hose team directed a solid stream of water into the basement windows.

A boisterous crowd gathered across the street to watch the excitement, several drunks among them held back by a couple of burly policemen wielding nightsticks. Some men broke into cheers when firemen axed through the front door of the building and snaked another hose into the building to attack the fire from the inside.

He'd seen enough. Dunn's lips curled in satisfaction as he closed the window and went back to bed. Means had done it. Tomorrow he would begin inquiries to learn the extent of the damage to the records. He slept soundly through the remainder of the night.

Two days passed before he got the answers he sought.

"They're certain it was a case of arson," the harried-looking senior files clerk said. "One of our junior men, a malcontent and a complainer, seems to be unaccounted for, and now some are blaming me. They say I'm remiss for not reporting him."

"They think he may have been responsible, then?"

"It appears suspicious, Mr. Dean. There is a strong smell of kerosene in the basement, and Mr. Means' desk was cleared of his personal belongings."

"Name's Dunn."

"Yes, yes. Beg pardon. Now, in answer to your question, all Surveyor General documents on the books since 1854 are ashes, completely ruined. We've no idea how to proceed. Someone will have to determine the names of those who have had surveys done and confirmed, the Congress will have to allocate the funds for new surveys, contracts to be let, and—oh, heavens, it's just a mess! Where to begin?" The harried man actually wrung his hands.

"I'm sorry for your trouble," Dunn said, feeling generous. "Isn't there anything remaining?"

"Well, yes, I suppose. The books containing records of Spanish Land Grant documents were untouched by fire or water. Odd, it was almost as if whoever set the fire deliberately removed them to a closet at the other end of the basement for safekeeping."

Taking his pocket watch from his waistcoat, Dunn apologized. "I must be going. I've taken too much of your valuable time. Good day, sir."

Another piece of Dunn's plan had fallen into place. Mr. Means had delivered on his promise. David Stone's legal claim to the land had gone up in smoke! Left unburned, the Spanish Land Grant documents—considered not legally binding by the Territorial government—ceding the grant lands to Esperanza Stone's father, were all that remained. Officially, those grant documents were the only record attached to 4,000 acres of land, and, more to the point, the water on and under the land.

There was much to be done, but first, a congratulatory drink. Dunn walked a few short blocks and entered the bar favored by the bureaucrats of the Territorial government for privacy and for its plush and overdone décor befitting any gentlemen's club back east. He stood at the bar savoring a premium whiskey, his mind racing. First, send a telegram to a discreet fellow in Albuquerque. Dunn didn't think the idea of blackmail might occur to Mr. Means, but just in case it did, timely action taken now would ensure the man's silence—permanently.

Next, have his lawyer draw up the papers, then file a claim of pre-emption to appear as a notice in the back pages of the newspaper. After six months, if it were uncontested, the claim would give the petitioner, one Franklin Dunn, title to the land. Dunn knew that what he intended to do was illegal, that a little-known clause in the land pre-emption law limited it to only quarter-sections of land, but most people were ignorant of that clause, and he counted on that lack of knowledge to get what he wanted. The Rocas Duras was far larger than the 160 acres that made up a quarter-section.

Stillwell's boys had bungled the job on Stone, and another attempt at killing him might attract too much attention. Dunn had to try a different approach. He was certain that David Stone would never learn of the claim, would fail to challenge it, and so, with a bit of sleight of hand on Dunn's part, would forfeit his ranch and all the stock on it. He would make sure that Stone's hands were full, and he'd have no time for newspapers. Besides, Dunn had spent freely to buy enough influence around Santa Fe so that no one there would interfere. Finally, by marrying the beautiful Beatriz, he could sew up his claim with the legitimacy of a family member, then begin his own family to establish his dynasty.

"Not bad for a boy no one wanted or thought had any potential at all. Not bad, Franklin my boy. Not bad at all." A caustic laugh escaped his lips, and passersby turned in surprise to see the stranger laughing to himself.

Chapter Twenty-two

The sun was well up as Cam and three of Pickett's men pushed the bawling cattle across the Texas plain many miles southwest of the panhandle town of Tascosa.

"Don't know how so few cattle can raise so much dust," Cam grumbled as his old nag, Dolly, slowly followed the other riders.

"Can't that hoss go any faster?" one of Pickett's men chided Cam. "I think you can walk faster than Dolly can run." The men had a laugh at Cam's expense. They didn't mind seeing him put down a level or two. Cam's ways were not their ways.

The men had located the cattle the day before and bunched them in a dry wash, where they had held them until sundown. Under the light of a pale moon they started the stolen cattle moving through a long night.

"Cam, get that steer circling back."

Cam grumbled but did what the men told him. "I got it." Cam turned the animal back to join the little herd. The men were tired and sweaty, but the steers required their constant attention. There were always a few breaking away, trying to circle back to their home range. When that happened, one of the drovers had to head the animals off and haze them back into line.

"Wear 'em out, and they'll settle down to the drive in a day or so," a man who called himself Red River Doc said to Cam.

Bitter dust hung heavy in the air, and, like the other men, Cam had pulled his bandana up to cover his mouth and nose. "Where are we taking them?"

"Our place. It's called Los Portales, over by Fort Stanton."

"But that's in New Mexico Territory, several days from here!"

"That's where the buyer is, boy."

"We've got maybe forty or fifty head here. Are they worth the drive all that far?"

Doc's eyes swept quickly over the moving mass of cattle. "We got fifty-five, all steers, all three or four years old, and they'll bring close to eight hundred dollars."

"How'd you do that?" Cam's eyes widened at the man's quick assessment of the stock.

"You talk too much, boy. You got work to do. Get back there behind the herd, and keep 'em from straggling."

Several days later Cam found that their destination, the place called Los Portales, was a bowl-shaped depression several hundred feet in diameter formed by a sinkhole in the limestone rock lying below the surface. The sink was way up a side draw off a long canyon. The sides of the hole were layers of dark gray rock four feet high and nearly vertical, making a natural holding pen for cattle.

At one part of the rim a small cave in a jumble of rocks provided some protection from the elements for several men and their gear. It was well known, and Lincoln County rustlers often used it as a place to hold stolen cattle for rebranding.

The branding filled out a hard day's work, but late in the morning Cam had a bit of trouble with the branding irons.

"Ain't you ever done any branding, boy?"

Cam had seen branding done back on his father's ranch. "I guess I watched more than actually took part."

"Didn't want to get your clothes dirty, I bet," one of the men razzed him.

Cam hesitated to tell them that this was his first time wrestling with the big steers his fellow rustlers roped and dragged close to where the irons lay in a fire.

By the end of the day, Cam was sweat-soaked, dirty, and exhausted, his face red from the heat of the fire. He'd burned a hole in one pant leg and sported a welt he got when an angry steer fought him and caused the hot iron to brush his skin.

"This is hardly worth it," Cam complained, although a part of him was proud to have made it through the day in one piece.

"You done good, for a rich boy. Maybe some grit in

you after all." Doc, the leader of their group, handed him a cup of coffee as Cam fell onto a nearby rock to regain his breath and rest his aching muscles.

The work done, the cattle milled nearby, now the responsibility of a couple of drovers who came with the buyer. Cam sipped the steaming coffee while the other two rustlers found some shade and leaned against a rock, hats tilted down over their eyes, legs stretched out before them. Doc talked with the buyer.

"Who are those men Doc's talking to?"

"The tall one's Donnelley, from over White Oak way," the rustler called Hub said from under his hat, "and the other man goes by Stillwell. He's from the high country west of Lincoln. But don't put much stock in names. Men have been known to change handles, depending."

"Depending on what?"

"On who's asking questions."

"Since the drive is over, do we get paid now?"

"We do, kid, but you don't. Doc says you still owe Pickett a heap of money."

"Yeah," the other rustler chuckled, "and I reckon you're gonna have to push many a steer to settle your account."

"So what do we do now?"

"Do? Why, now we'll just look around and find us a few cows to drive back to Texas and sell 'em over there."

"Boy," Hub said, "was you born yesterday?"

"Aw, Doc said he's a greenhorn, so what'd you expect?"

Doc and the buyer closed the deal, and Doc joined his small crew of rustlers near the fire. He poured himself a cup of coffee, took a swallow, then tossed the liquid into the fire with a bitter oath. He pulled out a sack of tobacco and papers and rolled a cigarette. He produced a match, used a thumbnail to scratch the match into flame, lit the cigarette, shook the match to extinguish it, and tossed it aside.

"What's doing, Doc?"

"Yeah." Hub spoke up. "Bad news?"

Cam looked from face to face, wondering what could be wrong.

"Donnelley said there's a new sheriff—a big fellow, and handy with a gun. Says he'll not be bought off, and he's making things hot for anybody that don't walk his line."

"And who might this feller be?"

"Name's Garrett," Doc said, tossing his cigarette butt into the fire. "Runs the hotel next to the White Elephant Saloon down in Lincoln."

"I've had a drink or two in there but never heard of him." Hub spat.

"Well, he's heard of us," Doc said. "He's saying that he's got his sights on Los Diablos, and he won't rest until he sees us in jail or in hell, and he don't care which."

"Yeah?" Hub said. "Talk is cheap. He don't scare me."

"Maybe you ought to be scared. Maybe all of us should. Donnelley said this Garrett is dancing to the tune played by the Territorial Governor."

"You mean Wallace?"

"That's right."

Cam remained quiet. He had read about Governor Wallace's attempts to end lawlessness in the Territory, especially in Lincoln County, with an offer of blanket amnesty for rustlers and other lawbreakers. That new sheriff sounded dangerous. Could Cam stay alive until he squared things with Pickett?

"Let's ride, boys. We got work to do, and I reckon Pickett's got to hear about this new sheriff."

Chapter Twenty-three

Several weeks of pushing rustled stock between the Texas panhandle caprock, across a wide belt of old sand dunes covered with scrub oak to the Pecos River and high, rolling hills north and west of Fort Stanton in New Mexico Territory had toughened Cam to the rugged outdoor life. He became ever more like those he rode with, rough and dangerous men who stole cattle for a living, his face burned by sun and wind and his hands calloused from the work. When Cam managed a rare shave, using a broken piece of mirror borrowed from Doc, the face that looked back at him showed a deep tan on his lower cheeks and from the end of his nose to his chin. Above that, where his hat protected him from the sun, his skin remained light.

There was no regular cook in the gang, so the men

survived on a diet of beans or corn dodgers and sometimes the meat of an antelope or mule deer unlucky enough to stray near them. They had beef only when a steer died along the trail or broke a leg and couldn't keep up. The other men had a chance to get to Tascosa or Lincoln for a meal and a night of drinking and carousing when they drew their pay, but Cam never did. Pickett came and went when they were pushing stolen cattle, making sure Cam stayed in camp, broke.

Cam rode his turn on watch around a herd they'd bedded down at Los Portales. Doc came through the darkness of a moonless night.

"I'll relieve you now, Stone. Go get some sleep while you can."

"Sure, Doc. Real quiet out tonight." Cam's night horse, a veteran pony that knew his role well enough, made his way back to the camp. Cam wondered if Pickett had asked his father for money. Would Pickett tell him if he'd written? Could Cam trust Pickett? Why should the man tell Cam anything? He had Cam working like an indentured servant, until *he* said the debt was paid. Cam stripped his gear from the pony and made his way in the darkness at the edge of camp to his bedroll, crawled under his blanket, and fell asleep.

Sometime later he was awakened by voices—had somebody spoken his name? Pickett and a pale, wasted-looking man sat by the fire, drinking whiskey from tin coffee cups and talking.

"Dunn's got it in his mind to have that girl and the RD too," the skinny man said, succumbing to a fit of deep, chest-rattling coughing. He hawked, turned his head, and spat, wiping his mouth on a shirtsleeve. He drank more whiskey to suppress the cough.

The RD? His father's ranch? What girl? Cam could see beads of sweat on the man's face glistening in the firelight. Who was this Dunn?

"You seen a doctor about that cough? You're sounding like a lunger to me."

"Naw, it's just something I picked up in a Texas *juzgado.* Their lockup weren't a healthy place."

"Well, that Dunn swings a wide loop," Pickett said, "but that won't change nothing. He'll still be buying as many steers as I can send his way."

The pale man took the proffered bottle, poured a dollop into his cup, drank from it, and suppressed another fit of coughing but said nothing.

"What's on your mind?" Pickett asked.

"I ain't so sure. He says he won't be the little man no more, once he's got that ranch."

"What do you mean by that?"

"I figure he's going to go on the up-and-up. Sees himself as a respectable rancher, an honest citizen."

"You mean he won't be moving rustled cattle for me?"

"He's worried about that sheriff. He's looking to get out while he can, make his spread like one of those big outfits, maybe even sell shares back east."

"Sell me out?" Pickett demanded. "I'll not stand for that."

"You got no choice, man."

"That's where you're wrong, Stillwell. If Dunn crosses me, I'll clean him out." Pickett rose, pacing before the fire. "Me and the boys will take every cow Stone has, then we'll round up Dunn's stock. We'll push half of 'em over to Texas and half up to Denver. Sure, he may get Stone's ranch, but there won't be a cow on it!"

"Dunn'll never stand for that."

"Well, me and the boys will knock him in the head and throw him into one of those bottomless lakes over toward the Pecos," Pickett said with a vicious oath, "and I'll take that ranch and maybe even this girl, after I see her for myself."

Stillwell stood, stretched, and said, "I'd best be getting back before sunrise."

As the two men talked, Cam's mind raced. So, Pickett *did* intend to go after his father's cattle. The man Stillwell, the sick one—he knew a lot about a fellow named Dunn. Cam had never seen him before and didn't remember meeting anybody named Dunn. Then again, Cam hadn't been around home much of late, and when he had been, he cared little about anyone back there. If his brother had mentioned Dunn, Cam had paid little attention. Now it appeared that this Dunn had made a business of selling rustled cattle, and *he* had designs on the Stone family ranch.

What girl had the man talked about? Cam knew that Beatriz had quite a following. But surely not!

Cam had to get away. He had to do something. But what?

Chapter Twenty-four

"Mrs. Stone, hope I'm not interrupting. Young James let me in on his way out and said you were in the kitchen. By the way, he said to tell you that he's taking Rojo for a ride." Hermann Krell stood at the kitchen door, hat in hand. "That's a young man who'd never leave the saddle if he didn't have to."

Esperanza nodded. "From what I see, he takes after Mr. Wagner that way." She waited to hear what Hermann wanted. He was a German farmer who rarely had time to stop for a social call unless he had a good reason.

"I need to see Mr. Stone. Is he around?"

"He's over on the east section with Mr. Wagner, but they should be getting back any time now. Do you want to have a cup of coffee while you wait?"

"No, ma'am, but thank you. I'll head out to see if I can find them." Hermann started out the door. "Thanks again." He stopped. "Oh, the missus asked me to see if you'd heard anything of Cam lately. She prays for him every night. I think he was always her favorite."

Esperanza sighed. "I appreciate the prayers, and ask Hilde to keep them up, but, no, we have heard nothing for several months."

Hermann left. As he rode past the barns, he saw David, Tilman, and Juan Javier approaching.

"Hermann! This is a pleasure. You remember Tilman Wagner." David rode up to the paddock in order to get off his horse. He was better, but the wound he'd incurred still hurt after a day in the saddle.

Juan Javier took all three horses and gave the reins to one of the hands. "What brings you over here this afternoon, Mr. Krell? Usually you're hard at work this time of the year with your orchards."

"Yes, but I had to show you and your father something I saw in the Santa Fe paper this week. It must be a mistake." Hermann pulled the paper from his pocket and handed it to David. Pointing to the unusually fine print, hardly legible, in the bottom left corner of a back page, he asked, "What do you make of that?"

David read aloud, "Pre-emption Notice. By order of the Chief Clerk responsible for pre-emptions from Division G, Private Land Claims Division, be it known that Frederick Dent claims ownership of a certain tract of land, containing,"—he paused and held the paper up close to his eyes. "I can't read this. Looks like an ink blot or something, but I can't tell how many acres it is."

"Well," Krell said, "we couldn't read it either."

David continued. "Uh, such and such a number of acres, more or less, 'sections 16 through'—I can't read this number either—uh, 'township 23 North, range 9 East, of the Pecos River meridian. The facts are substantially these: Prior to the survey of said township, the said Dent, a citizen of the United States, over the age of 21 years and qualified pre-emptor, while prospecting for a home upon the unsurveyed lands of the United States subject to pre-emption, or that might so become when the same should be surveyed, settled on this land, formerly contained in a grant from the Spanish throne, since ruled null and void, and, intending to claim the same as pre-emptor, was on said land at the date of Federal survey in 1878.' " David's shoulders slumped. "What is this? We had no survey done in 1878."

"Walter found this," Hermann said. "The location was familiar, so he checked our deeds. When he showed it to me, I knew you'd want to know."

"This fellow Dent," Tilman asked, "who's he?"

"Never heard of him," David said.

"Papá, that sounds like the Rocas Duras. Is this legal? What does it mean?"

"Walter said it reads like the Homestead Act," Hermann said, "but maybe you need a lawyer."

Tilman squinted at the article and turned to David. "Didn't you tell me that Esperanza's father had taken care of this grant and placed it in both your names and made sure it met all the necessary requirements for the new Territories?"

"He did, Tilman. Esperanza's father was a smart businessman. He knew that this would be prime land because of the water and location." He turned to Hermann. "I don't know what's going on. Who could be doing this?" David was confused by this turn of events. "Why?"

Juan Javier saw that his father was shaken by the notice and tried to cover his father's weakness. "Thank you, Mr. Krell. We'll look into this immediately."

Hermann got back onto his horse. "You are a good neighbor. There have been too many accidents lately. I figure someone is out to get your land, one way or another." He turned his horse and headed for home.

Tilman held the notice. "Krell's right. You need a lawyer. Let's talk tonight, and y'all can ride for Socorro tomorrow and see what Baca can find out about this mess."

David hesitated, eyes downcast. "I don't know, Tilman. I'm short of cash right now."

"You're always short of cash, Papá. Cam has taken every extra dime you have, and now we are all going to suffer for it, aren't we?"

"Juan Javier, behave. Cam is still your brother."

"I know Papá, but we spend a lot more time worrying about Cam then he does worrying about us, I think." Juan Javier turned away and headed to his small house. "I must go. Patricia will be wondering what happened to us." He headed down the path, aiming a kick at a calico barn cat in his anger.

Tilman stopped David. "Catherine and I have done

well with some mining investments, and we will be more than happy to help. We are family, you know."

David was quiet. "I hope that won't be necessary. Anyway, Santa Rosa has a notarized copy of the deed and confirmation locked away in his vault. Juan Javier and I will go tomorrow to Socorro."

"How long will that take you?"

"The Army road from Fort Stanton to Fort Craig—the one you came here on, Tilman—is a good one, and we can go quickly. We will speak with my son-in-law. He will know a trustworthy lawyer, and we shall see what we can do about this."

Chapter Twenty-five

The single-hitched, high-stepping mare moved the light runabout along at an easy trot. The "road" was actually two cleared tracks worn by iron wagon wheels and for the first few miles sloped gradually downhill through rolling hills thickly covered with grama grass. Tilman let James drive, noting with satisfaction that the boy held the reins as his four-and six-in-hand stage-driving friend Butter Pegram had taught him in Colorado. It was a cool, clear morning, and both Tilman and James squinted when the sun cleared the eastern hills in what promised to be a cloudless blue sky.

A large mule-deer buck stood on a nearby rise, watching until they passed. Along the way they saw a few cattle here and there carrying David's brand. Not many, but enough for Tilman to figure that there must be even more back in the brush up some draw, half wild and wary of any man.

By midmorning their track intercepted a well-worn military road, and James took the fork to the right to cross a wooden bridge over the Rio Bonito. The crystal-clear waters, perhaps fifteen feet wide but only a few feet deep, rushed past as father and son continued on a short distance until the orderly, whitewashed stone and adobe buildings of Fort Stanton came into view.

"What kind of a place is this we're coming to?" James asked.

"An Army fort," Tilman answered.

"I never saw one before. Do they have soldiers here?"

"Your Uncle David told me there are. But these are different, like the ones we saw in the mountains before we got to the Stones' house. They're like the ones I saw at Fort Davis in Texas last year, when Butter and I went to help my friend Captain Law."

"Why are they different?"

"They're cavalry, but they belong to colored regiments, the ones the Indians call Buffalo Soldiers because of their dark skin."

"Will we see any of them?"

"I reckon we will," Tilman answered.

"Why are they way out here? Who do they fight?"

"They used to fight Indians, but nowadays they don't have to do that."

"Dad, were you ever a soldier?"

"I was, but a long time ago. And I walked everywhere I went"—Tilman chuckled—"and carried everything I owned wrapped in a blanket across my shoulder. Now, my friend John, a fellow I grew up with—he had his own horse, so he got to be a cavalryman."

"What did you do?"

"I'll tell you all about it when you're a little older."

The buildings of Fort Stanton, home to the black soldiers of the 9th U.S. Cavalry Regiment (Colored), surrounded the usual vast parade ground marked by a flagpole in the center. Tilman pointed out the post sutler's store down a dusty street past the long, low stables and corrals, and James pulled the mare to a halt.

"Son, cool her off before you let her have any water. Wait for me over there," Tilman said, pointing to a nearby cottonwood grove across the road from the fort.

"Yes, sir," James said.

The wait proved to be one of several hours' duration. James found the bugle calls and comings and goings of the cavalrymen new and fascinating, but not for long. The food basket Catherine had placed in the runabout drew the boy's attention. Lifting the cloth cover, James rummaged around to pull out a sandwich with thick slices of beef, a jar of water, and two *empanadas*. After eating all that, he fished out still another *empanada* to satisfy his hunger.

A comfortable place in the shade under a cottonwood tree beckoned. Leaning against the massive trunk, James opened the pocketknife Butter had given him and played mumblety-pegs. When the regimental band assembled for practice and began tooting away, marching this way and that, James put away the knife to enjoy the show. James saw Tilman and two other men leave a building marked COMMISSARY and go into a smaller building with a bigger sign, POST HEADQUARTERS. The sun was midway down the afternoon sky when Tilman returned.

"Let's go home, son."

"Did you see them riding in lines?" James asked as they got into the runabout.

"Those were drills," Tilman explained. "They were practicing how to move on a battlefield. When they first get to where the enemy is, they're in column of twos or fours. Then they have to shift around and spread out into a line to fight."

"Do you know how to do that?" an excited James asked.

"Not the way cavalry does it. I was a soldier who walked. We did some of the same moves, only on foot."

After many questions about a soldier's life, James finally exhausted himself, falling asleep and leaning against Tilman's side under his protective arm, oblivious to the rough road.

The sun slipped behind the western mountains, casting long shadows across the RD. James awoke and unhitched the mare and hung the harness, grabbing handfuls of fresh straw. He rubbed down the mare and hurriedly poured her a bait of grain. He ran to tell his mother all he had seen that day.

Tilman, David, and Juan Javier took their coffee into the library. On the *pórtico* in the cool of the evening, Catherine and Esperanza sat in wicker chairs and sipped their coffee, eavesdropping through the library's open window without appearing to do so.

"Santa Rosa has the legal documents on the RD." David summed up his visit to Socorro for Tilman's benefit. "One of the bank's lawyers will review everything, and if it goes to court, we've got a solid case."

"But we're still cash poor," Juan Javier said. "A long, drawn out court case could sink us in legal fees."

"I have bad news. I spoke with the commissary officer at the fort today," Tilman said. "His beef, pork, and hay contracts for the post are filled. The same goes for the Mescalero Apache Agency contracts. All filled."

David's shoulders slumped. Juan Javier was stolid, his eyes hooded. On the *pórtico,* Esperanza's eyes closed as she squeezed Catherine's hand.

"But it's not all bad," Tilman said.

"How so?" David asked. "We've no market, and even if we did, most of my men are gone. The few of us left can't scare up enough cattle to put together a herd to sell."

"Not so fast. The commissary officer showed me a letter dated last week. It came from a fellow in El Paso. He's looking for beef and has a contract to supply the surveyors and work crews doing some grading work for the El Paso and Northeastern Railroad that's going to pass to the east of us. He also told me about one of the big companies in White Oaks, where the rep is looking to buy meat for company miners. There must be close to three thousand folks in White Oaks these days, and they've got to eat."

"White Oaks must be like Mahonville—I mean, Vista Buena. It's full of miners," Catherine whispered to Esperanza.

Tilman continued. "Seems the rustlers hit pretty hard over there, and this fellow came up short on his contracts. He's got to feed the gold miners, and he'll take as many head as we can deliver, *if* we can get there in a month. How far is it? Maybe forty miles or so, right? The Army says they pay top dollar." Tilman put his coffee cup on a side table. "Those buyers need beef and can afford to pay for it. You've got beef back in the hills, and you can use the money."

"We may have missed a few wild ones at the roundup," David said, his voice toneless, weary with defeat, "but I don't know if we can get enough."

"Papá, this is our chance," Juan Javier said. "We must try."

"But Dunn said we could sell our beef to that buyer in Las Vegas," David protested, afraid to give up a given for a potentially unknown solution.

"I'm not so sure about why he made that offer," Tilman said. "I'd feel a lot better about driving a herd to White Oaks than Las Vegas. Where are we going to find water for the herd on that Las Vegas route? There's a reason old Chisum uses the Goodnight-Loving Trail along the Pecos River when he drives a herd to Trinidad and Denver. What does he know that we don't?"

"We know there's water for the herd between here and White Oaks," David said. "So if we go that route, we can move a herd slowly so as not to run the fat off of them—take maybe a week to do it." Hope lifted the terrible weight of impending failure from David's shoulders. "Tilman, will you act as boss on this drive?"

"If that's what you want, sure. It'll take some doing, but we'll go cow hunting and pop every wily old bull, steer, cow, and calf out of the brush, no matter how far back in the hills they've gone," Tilman said. "If it has to be a mixed herd, so be it. We'll quarter your range, move a chuck wagon out there, and sweep a quarter at a time."

"And I'll go talk to Mr. Chisum, Papá. We can mortgage a few head from him. If we can put together maybe five hundred, we can pay him off and have enough to keep us going."

"All right," Tilman said, taking out a tally book and pencil stub. "We've got thirty days from today to gather a herd and get it to White Oaks. If it takes, say, five days to drive 'em from here, then that means we have to start 'em in just over three weeks from now. We can't afford to waste any time, so we'll plan this thing and get started."

"My husband! My son!" Esperanza exclaimed, rushing into the room, her smile radiant. "You can do this!"

"Esperanza? Where did you come from?" He glanced

at the open window, where the fluttering curtains gave away the women's eavesdropping place. "I might have known."

"Wine!" Juan Javier called. "We will drink to our success!"

Chapter Twenty-six

After five hard days pushing cattle on the range, the men knocked off work for a few hours. A bath, a shave, and shucking salt- and dust-encrusted clothes for clean ones proved a welcome respite from days in the saddle. Following Sunday dinner the family gathered outdoors under the sunny afternoon skies to talk, a chance to bring the women up to date on their progress. Juan Javier sat on a *banco,* an ornately carved wooden chair, by the inner courtyard wall. He had been unusually quiet during the meal, saying only, "We must talk."

Everyone sat except David, who leaned on his cane, saying, "I ate too much, and I've got to stand." He kept it to himself that his wound was slow to heal, wrapping it when no one could see. The hard riding was taking more of a toll on him than he acknowledged.

"We ought to start the herd in a week, but we're still

a couple of hands and a lot of cattle short." Juan Javier confronted his father and Tilman. "This is a large drive for so few of us, and we need all the help we can get. Now, the men say that Billy Bonney has been seen in White Oaks."

"I suppose that means that hands are afraid to sign on," Tilman grumbled, pushing his chair back and standing up. "We've ridden over a lot of range lately, but if there were any rustlers out there, we haven't seen them. Everybody knows the RD's been skinned as far as stock goes. There are bigger herds with fatter cattle elsewhere in the county, easier pickings than the stuff we've pushed out of the hills."

David listened and then said, "It makes me wonder if somebody isn't putting out scare talk to keep us shorthanded."

"I talked to a fellow in the sutler's store at Stanton the other day," Tilman said. "He told me that Bonney's been over around Fort Sumner sparking some girl, and if that's the case, I don't think he's looking to mess with any piddling little trail drive of ours." Tilman paused. "We'll work this out, boys." Before he could explain, old Santiago appeared in the gateway to the courtyard.

"*Viejo,*" David called to him, "what is it?"

"Riders, *patrón.*"

"I'll go see," Juan Javier said.

"We'll join you," David said.

Outside the courtyard the men watched as two riders wearing long linen dusters, their faces shaded by big hats, made their way up the road to the house. The riders drew up, and Tilman stepped forward, grinning in recognition. "Light and set!" he called.

Both riders dismounted, one a man of medium height who groaned a loud "Ahhh!" as he slapped his rear with both hands, and the other a woman six feet tall. Both shook dust from their hats.

"Figured you might need somebody to straighten you out." Butter Pegram reached out with one arm and gave the stately woman beside him a hug. "So we come a-runnin'." A girlish blush crept from beneath her neckerchief into the woman's cheeks.

"Mr. Pegram," she admonished, "not in front of everybody!"

Butter clearly relished the surprise on Tilman's face. "Ain't you going to introduce me to Catherine's relatives?"

"I'm sorry. Welcome, friend." Tilman gave Butter a handshake and hugged Neala. "I'm shocked, that's all. I thought you two were still on your honeymoon."

During introductions, the men were awkward at first when taking Butter's right hand with its missing forefinger.

Butter joked, "Don't mind my stub. It's all right. The last time I saw that whole finger was down near the Rio Grande, when a bunch of fellers was shootin' at me and Tilman."

"No!" Esperanza said, knowing a born storyteller when she heard one. "How terrible!"

"Well," Butter said, warming to his audience, "there

I was, surrounded, and did I mention we was about out of bacon and coffee?"

"And that's another story," Neala interrupted, "for another time."

"So," David said, "you are the man who befriended Tilman in Colorado and then followed him to Fort Davis last year."

"He's the one," Tilman said. "He came to help when renegades kidnapped my friend John Law's daughter and a schoolteacher."

"The honor is ours, Señor Pegram," Juan Javier said, glad that his father was finding some small relief from the pressing worries of the coming drive. "You must tell us all, for Tilman has kept his adventures to himself long enough."

Catherine took Neala by the hand. "I am so happy to meet the woman who stole this wonderful man's heart."

"I've heard much about you too," Neala said. "But I hope you don't mind our barging in like this." Neala patted Butter gently on the top of his head, causing the others to smile at the obvious affection the two shared. "Mr. Pegram insisted that you needed our help."

"Come on in out of the dust, and let's get you something to drink, and you can freshen up while the men talk," Esperanza said.

"I am so grateful to see you both." Catherine's eyes welled with tears. "We can never thank you enough."

Tilman snapped his fingers. "It was Catherine. *She* wrote to you, didn't she, Butter?"

"She said you all might need our help. Besides, who wants to honeymoon in San 'tone when you can lie out under a canopy of stars and rejoice in the Maker's glory?"

"Watch out, David. If he and Neala get to spouting that poetry stuff, we'll never get a word in."

David, emotion flooding over him, said, "You mean you and your beautiful wife have come to help us instead of going on a honeymoon?"

"What are friends for, Mr. Stone? Tilman and I have been through a lot, and when Catherine wrote and told us about your troubles, Neala didn't even hesitate. We just came." Patting Tilman on the back, Butter said, "And here we are."

"Mr. Butter! Mr. Butter!" James trotted up on Rojo, jumped off, and hugged Butter. "I'm so glad to see you!"

"James! Show me this beaut of a horse you're ridin'." Butter and James admired the horse, giving the others a moment to regain their composure.

"Catherine said he was a true friend," David said to Esperanza, "more like a brother."

Tilman followed Butter and James as they led the horse to the barn.

Later, after Butter and Neala cleaned up, Tomasa warmed up *carne asada,* or beef stew, and some tortillas left over from dinner. Coffee followed, with cinnamon-sprinkled pumpkin *empanadas,* and they sat around the table to talk about the latest news.

"We'll need a chuck wagon for the trail. Neala will

do the cooking." Butter was all business. "And I'll spell her with the driving. I reckon you can show me how to push cattle as well." He saw David start to speak and, guessing what was on his mind, held up a hand to stop him. "We'll take care of the grub and such and keep a tally that we'll settle up when we get to the end of the trail. That suit you, David?"

Esperanza spoke as she saw David try to speak and fail. "Thank you, Butter. That will work fine. We can never repay this kindness."

"Now see here, ma'am. You're our adopted family now, I'm afraid. Whether you like it or not." Butter patted Neala on the shoulder. "Ready for bed, punkin'?"

Tilman tried not to look at Catherine. *Punkin'?*

Neala rose gracefully. "I am tired. But if it's all right with Tomasa, I'd like to use the kitchen in the morning to make doughnuts for James. He heard a tall tale about them from Tilman, and I'm bound to show him the truth of it."

Laughing, she and Butter went off to Cam's room, leaving the rest of the family quiet with thought.

"Catherine, these things take time," Tilman said. "When did you write to Butter?"

"Before we left Colorado."

"What?"

"I'm sorry. I should have talked to you, but I knew Butter would want to help us."

"But they just got married," Tilman protested, his temper rising.

"So did we," Catherine said, not backing down.

Esperanza decided it was time to change the subject. "Well, it looks as if we'll be ready to go soon."

" 'We'?" David stood. "What do you mean 'we'?"

"We're going with you, David. It's my future as well as yours. Besides, Catherine and I are excellent shots and ride as well as any of you men. We'll be fine."

A bewildered David looked to Tilman for help, only to find him speechless.

Esperanza started to leave the room but stopped suddenly, dismay evident on her patrician face. "What was I thinking? Beatriz is due home in a week for the summer, and she will want to be right in the middle of this. I know her, and she will be more trouble than the cattle!" Esperanza sank to the chair beside David, leaning her head against his chest. "What will we do?"

"Why not let her stay with Graciela? They get along well, and she doesn't get away with as much there as when she is with us." David put his arms around Esperanza. "It must be done, for her safety. My son," David said, "Beatriz will understand if you go and explain to her why we must do this. I know she will."

"But, David—" Esperanza began.

"Esperanza, if you insist on going on the drive with us, we have got to do this."

"Papá," Juan Javier exclaimed, "how can I help if I am in Socorro?"

"Join us as soon as you can," David said. He spoke with more confidence than he felt. His world was spinning crazily. He had lost one son who should be here helping the family. Since he had been shot and nearly died, every day he thought how easily a man might lose his life. Always a strong man, these days David felt weak, afraid of losing everything and powerless to prevent it. Would he fail to protect Esperanza? Who were these new members of his family who had come here to help? And who were their friends? Could they prevail against the evil that sought to bring him down? Juan Javier, the dependable one, stood by him. But were they all strong enough?

Chapter Twenty-seven

"It isn't fair! I am not a child. I am a woman."

"Beatriz, listen to yourself. This is not a game our father is in."

"Oh, I know that, Graciela." Beatriz tossed a tortoiseshell comb to the floor, stomping one small foot in anger, wringing her hands in dismay. "But I can help on the trail drive." Beatriz sank into one of the overstuffed red love seats that decorated her sister-in-law's home. I ride better than most men. You know that. I could help."

Graciela's large Victorian-style home showcased many of the latest fads found on the pages of *Godey's Fashion Magazine.* The new house stood two stories tall, imposing and modern. It sat amid other well-to-do family homes in the rich farmland near the Rio Grande.

Trimmed with ornate gingerbread woodwork, the lacy façade suited the Bacas' style of life. It was not David and Esperanza's idea of beauty, but they knew Graciela loved it.

The town of Socorro was old but prosperous. Located on the Camino Real, a trade route between Santa Fe to the north and Zacatecas, Mexico, in the south, its nearby lead and silver mines drew people seeking riches from across the country.

Graciela's husband, Santa Rosa Baca, was a banker of some local standing. Quite a bit older than Graciela, he indulged her every whim. Graciela had always been an obedient child, but she possessed a weakness for the good things in life and had carefully chosen her husband with that thought in mind. It was a marriage that worked for both of them. She was an excellent hostess, and her parties and were prized social events in Socorro.

"We will have a wonderful time, *mi hermana querida.* I am going to have a grand fête next week. You can meet some of the eligible young men from the town and from the farms along the river." Graciela cajoled her younger sister, so beautiful and so flighty and so not like herself. Graciela adored Beatriz and would defend her against anyone. However, she couldn't protect her from herself, and these days Beatriz was her own worst enemy.

"Graciela, I don't want to meet any young men. I have Walter at home, and the mysterious Mr. Dunn seems to think I am not unattractive. He is fascinating, no?"

"Beatriz, stay away from Mr. Dunn. There is something about him that bothers me. Besides, he is quite a bit older than you."

Laughter broke the tension in the room. "Listen to yourself. How much older is your Santa Rosa than you, may I ask?"

"But there is so much difference between you and me, *querida.*" Graciela smiled in spite of her concern. "You are like quicksilver, while I am as solid as the rocks on our ranch."

Beatriz picked up the comb from the floor. "I think you are like the silent water of our ranch, Graciela. Necessary to all of us in order to survive." Hugging her sister, Beatriz departed for her room, her anger gone as quickly as it had come.

The following afternoon the sisters sat with Santa Rosa Baca in the dining room of La Casita, one of the small adobe hotels used for many years by travelers along El Camino Real. Santa Rosa had only minutes to spare from his busy schedule, so he downed his glass of wine and excused himself to return to his work at the bank.

"I am so glad we stopped at Mrs. Sloan's dressmaking shop. The new material she got in will make a wonderful present for Mother. She has wanted—"

"Ladies!"

Beatriz and Graciela looked up from their purchases into the cool eyes of Franklin Dunn. Wearing an expensive brown tweed jacket despite the warmth of the afternoon, Dunn looked every inch a gentleman. Still, Graciela thought him far too old for Beatriz.

"Mr. Dunn." Graciela nodded her head, not encouraging further conversation.

"What are you doing in Socorro?" a surprised Beatriz blurted.

"I had business in town and decided to spend an extra day here. What about you?"

Beatriz smiled with delight. "I am staying with my sister for a few days, and we decided to shop for some new fabric and stop for coffee and a sweet. Do you have time to join us?" She quickly reached for the purchases to make room, but Graciela was quicker, gathering the packages as she stood.

"I'm sorry, Mr. Dunn. We were just leaving. Beatriz forgets that I have a child at home who needs attention." Graciela gracefully started to leave, positioning herself between her younger sister and Franklin Dunn. "It was nice to see you."

"Oh, Graciela." Beatriz's lower lip drew into a pout, but, seeing her sister's warning look, she quietly followed, nodding as the waiter escorted them to the door, bowing, thanking them, and begging them to come back soon. Outside, the two young women turned and strolled down the street.

This was Dunn's chance to see Beatriz without all of her family around. Dunn didn't care for the cold, wary looks he always got from Juan Javier Stone. Pulling a fancy, engraved calling card and a pencil from his coat pocket, Dunn quickly wrote a note on the back. One of the young boys standing around the plaza came in response to his call and waited until he finished writing.

"That one, the younger one," Dunn said, placing a coin and the card in the boy's palm, "you follow her and give her the note—wait until she is alone. *¿Entiendes?*"

The youngster, nodding assent, pocketed the coin, setting off to follow the women.

Later in the afternoon, Beatriz went outside to where the groom held her horse for a ride and found a street boy waiting by Graciela's front gate.

"*Señorita,* wait."

Beatriz took a small card from the boy, who turned and ran in the direction of the town.

I will be at the San Miguel Church later this afternoon lighting a candle. I am sorry we had such a short visit earlier today. Perhaps—FD

Slipping the card into the pocket of her short riding jacket and holding her crop in one hand, Beatriz easily climbed the short step, placed her boot into the stirrup, and settled into the saddle seat. Her legs found the upper and lower pommels of the sidesaddle she always used in town as she took the reins from the groom. The church was surely a safe and respectable place. Walking the horse around by the kitchen, she saw Celestina, Graciela's cook, nodding off in a rocking chair on the back veranda, the sun's warmth easing aches in her old bones and joints.

"Celestina, I am going to the chapel to light a candle

for a safe trip for Mother and Father, and I'll be back shortly. *Adiós.*" Leaving Celestina no time for a rejoinder, Beatriz rode across the fields to the mission. She planned to be gone only a short time. Graciela would never know.

Thirty minutes later, Beatriz left the horse tied to a post by the mission and entered. She passed from the bright sunlight outside into the darker interior, where it was cool and quiet, taking a moment for her eyes to adjust. The leather heels of her riding boots echoed loudly on the terra-cotta tiles, attracting unwanted stares from a few people who knelt in prayer. Beatriz looked around, did not see Mr. Dunn, and went to light a candle. After praying, she sat in the back of the church, eyes closed. Her parents worried her. So much trouble with Cam, yet they kept their fears and concerns to themselves. Why were they trying so hard to protect her? Her father was recovering after being shot by horse thieves. Their cattle had been stolen. Would justice never come to her family?

She sniffed. *How inconsiderate! I am alone in this pew, but someone chooses to sit right next to me. And wearing such strong cologne for an afternoon.* She opened her eyes, surprised to see Mr. Dunn sharing her pew.

"So, you got my note," he whispered. "Come, let's go outside so we can talk."

Beatriz glanced at the other people but recognized no one, so she accompanied Dunn. The two stopped in the shade of the arches outside the chapel.

Dunn wasted no time. "I don't think your sister likes me very much."

"My sister is very protective of me, Mr. Dunn."

"Franklin, Beatriz. Surely we are on first-name terms by now." Franklin took her small hand in his.

How smooth are his hands! Her father and Juan Javier and Walter all had rough and calloused hands from hours of labor on the ranch and farm. Mr. Dunn must do little manual work.

"Why don't we go sit by the fountain and talk? We never have a moment to ourselves."

Flattered in spite of herself, Beatriz allowed Dunn to lead her to the center of the mission grounds to sit. "I can't stay long. Graciela will—"

"Surely you can stay a few minutes." Franklin patted her hand, but Beatriz nervously withdrew it from his. "Where are your parents, by the way? I haven't seen them for a week or so."

"I'm not sure. They had some business with the cattle, I think. I really must be going soon, Mr. Dunn." For some reason, Beatriz hesitated, reluctant to tell Franklin more. Why? She didn't know. This meeting was to be a lark, but the man was looking at her in a way that made her uncomfortable.

"Surely you aren't afraid of me, are you, Beatriz? I'm perfectly harmless."

As harmless as a fox outside the chicken coop. "Of course I'm not afraid of you." Why would he not stop looking at her that way?

Franklin laughed. "I have admired you ever since I met you, and I hope to be able to make my intentions known to your father when he returns. When did you say that would be?"

"I don't know." *Intentions?* What was he talking about? She should not be alone with him. She stood to go, but Franklin placed a hand on her shoulder, stopping her.

"Why are you in such a hurry? You have flirted and preened and done everything possible to make sure I noticed you. Why play the innocent now?"

"I don't know what you're talking about, Mr. Dunn. Please let me go. Graciela will be worried if I don't return soon."

"You know what I'm talking about, my girl, and I won't be made a fool of. Your innocent act doesn't deceive me in the least." Dunn fought to hold his temper. He hated playing the fool to anyone, and he intended to show Beatriz Stone who was in charge.

"Beatriz! There you are. I was on my way home and saw your horse." Santa Rosa Baca appeared at her side and gently pulled her to him. "Mr. Dunn. How nice to see you. You are here for prayers as well?"

Franklin took a deep breath, controlling his emotions. "Why, yes, Señor Baca. I happened to encounter Beatriz and was inquiring about her family."

"How neighborly. Well, I am sorry to impose, but Beatriz must get home, as Graciela is having company tonight and needs her help. It was good to see you." Without missing a step, Santa Rosa escorted the visibly shaken Beatriz to her horse, and they were on their way.

"How did you know?" Beatriz asked when she regained her composure.

"You are not very good at assignations, my dear. You dropped the note on the ground when you left Celestina."

"But . . . how?" Her fingers probed but found an empty jacket pocket.

Baca smiled. "It must have fallen out. God protected you. Anyway, Celestina gave the card to Graciela, who sent the stable boy to the bank, and here I am. Your rescuer."

"Oh, Santa Rosa. I was so foolish. I don't like that man. He is much different than I thought. I will tell you something else I noticed."

"What, young lady?" Santa Rosa rode beside her, admiring the return of her confidence but at the same time glad she was David and Esperanza's daughter, not his.

"For a rancher, that man has never done much work himself. His hands are like a woman's." Beatriz blushed. Bankers didn't have rough hands either. "You know what I mean."

They both laughed as they rode up to the house. It looked beautiful to Beatriz. She had learned a lesson today and would be more careful in the future.

"Listen to me, Beatriz. Stay close to us until your parents return." Santa Rosa slowed his horse, thinking. *Strange. How is it that Franklin Dunn has the soft hands of a banker if he's always been a rancher?* "I don't think I trust that man either. Something doesn't ring true."

"I agree, Santa Rosa. Thank you. Graciela is a lucky woman."

As if she heard her name, Graciela stepped outside, glad to see her sister safe but ready to tell her a few things about proper behavior.

Chapter Twenty-eight

"Doc, I've had enough of eating dust and chousing steers," Cam said. "It's been too long since I had a bath and a shave, a decent meal, a drink, or put my arms around a pretty woman."

"Boss said you ain't to leave the camp," Doc warned.

"Well, it's inhuman what he wants from me, and I'll bust if I stay here another day," Cam said, picking up his saddle and gear. "I'm going to see a little lady down Mesilla way, and when I'm good and ready, I'll be back." He patted the pistol he carried in a holster on his hip. "And if Pickett wants some of this, he'll get it!"

Doc laughed. "About time, boy. I was beginning to wonder if you had any sand in your craw or if you were going to let Pickett push you around all your life. Get on out of here!"

Cam roped his favorite pony out of the remuda while

Doc helped himself to another cup of coffee. "Doc, I reckon I've taken about as much as any man can stand. I'll not back water for Pickett nor anyone else."

"Cam, a real man will back only as far as the air behind him. You've grown, and I figure you'll do to ride with."

Swinging into his saddle, Cam felt good about Doc's compliment. He'd had few enough of those of late. He rode until the camp lay behind him a couple of miles to the north and, well out of sight of anyone, swung in a wide westerly loop before settling into his intended direction—north. Mesilla lay in the opposite direction. He'd told Doc the wrong place in case anyone decided to head after him. He hated to lie to the one man who'd treated him as an equal, but this was something he had to do. Across those mountains far to his front, Santa Fe nestled in a wide valley, and his pony fell into a lively trot, eager to be on the trail.

Cam knew of only one way out of the fix he'd created for himself. If he could pull it off, he might have a chance to make things right. An image of his mother and father came to mind. He saw them sitting at the table with Tomasa bustling around them, sometimes scolding and sometimes laughing with the family. Cam missed those days, even if at times they had appeared dull. A hard teacher, life. It made Cam realize what he had so carelessly thrown away.

Trouble lay behind, and more trouble awaited him ahead, but the freedom of the open range called to the young man. He breathed deeply of the cool, fresh air from the mountains, the wind flavored with the sweet smell of piñon, the sky clear in the brilliant sunshine. It was a good day to be a man, full of youthful strength and purpose.

"I'll not be mistreated," he said aloud. "I'll not be made a fool of by any man!"

Cam spoke both Spanish and English fluently, and his mind slipped easily between the two languages. Santa Fe in his mind became The City of Holy Faith. Savoring the sounds and smells of the bustling city around him, Cam walked his pony through the streets of the town. The adobe buildings seemed to grow from the earth. In truth, they were a *part* of the earth. He was at home.

Once, in a Mesilla *cantina,* men at the bar beside Cam had spoken of a miraculous staircase at the Loretto Chapel in Santa Fe. Built with no visible supports, it yet allowed the sisters to reach the choir loft without ladders. Cam wanted to see this wonder for himself.

Asking directions, he made his way through the town. He hitched his horse outside the ornately carved sandstone chapel, which was a rich, buttery tan in color with an inlaid stained-glass window above the door. With the brashness of his youth Cam strode into the quiet sanctuary to look at the staircase, intent only on satisfying his curiosity. It was a mystery, and Cam stared, trying to understand it. The wooden staircase made two complete 360-degree turns, reaching nearly twenty feet between the floor and the choir loft. He counted thirty-three steps, the risers even, perfectly spaced, with no center support. Why did it stand without collapsing?

He must tell Mamá about this miracle. For the first time in years he felt a stirring deep inside him. He found a pew, to rest. A man ought to study the stairs. The quiet of the place reassured him, somehow, that his mission was just.

Later, at peace with his decision, he found a stable for his horse and up the street a cheap hotel with a restaurant alongside. His poke was near empty, but Cam figured he was good for a couple of days if he was careful. The hotel clerk gave Cam directions to a barbershop that offered a bath and had a washwoman who would also mend a rip in his faded old jeans.

By late afternoon, his clothes clean if threadbare, Cam explored the Territorial capitol. *Siesta* time was over, the businesses fronting the streets reopened, and men were out to see, the women to be seen. Cam's walk along the increasingly crowded streets took him past the governor's office, and after a moment's hesitation he walked into the building.

Across the foyer a lean, heavily mustached man of medium height talked with a bookish-looking younger man. Cam approached, and the two turned to look at him.

"Where can I find the governor?"

"Look here, you've got to have an appointment to see the governor." The young man bristled.

"Well, who do I see to do that?"

"You come and see me tomorrow. The president's rewarded the governor with an ambassadorship for ending the Lincoln County War, and he'll be leaving soon," the young man said self-importantly. "His time is valuable."

"Now, Perkins," the older man said, "don't treat this fellow like that." Turning to Cam, he offered his hand, looking him over as he spoke. "I'm Governor Wallace, and I've still a few days remaining in office. What can I do for you?"

"My name is Carlos Abram Minear Stone. Folks call me Cam for short, sir. I'm from Lincoln County." Cam paused, took a deep breath, and continued. "I'm here to tell you it's not completely cleaned up, and I've got a big problem only you can help me fix."

"Step into my office, and we'll talk," Wallace said. "Perkins, see we're not interrupted."

"But, Governor, your dinner reservations . . ."

"Can wait. Call for a pot of coffee for us."

Governor Wallace took his seat behind a massive desk, waving Cam into one of two chairs opposite him. He wasted no time. "Tell me, young Mr. Stone, what you mean."

Cam found Wallace to be a no-nonsense sort of man and one whose interest in Cam's problems seemed genuine. "It's this way, sir. I've got myself into a pile of trouble, and I don't know how to get out. I'm not too proud of what I done with my life so far. I've done things that my folks never taught me, and I've made a pretty bad mess of things. I tried to take the easy way out, and now I'm paying for it big-time."

"Tell me who you're working with, Cam."

"I've been doing some cattle rustling for Charlie Pickett. I owed him money and knew my folks were about played out, so I took a deal to pay my way out. He was supposed to request money from my father, but I know now he never planned on doing that. He's working with a man called Dunn, and they're planning on stealing from my father as well. I can't have that, sir."

"Is your father the Stone who owns the Rocas Duras in Lincoln County?"

"Yes, sir. He's a fine man, and I've done poorly by him, I'm afraid." Cam paused. "But I'm not foolish enough to let my family be wiped out by these no-accounts I'm working for. I know I did wrong, but I don't know how to get out of this mess and help my family too."

Cam spoke at length, interrupted several times by the governor, who asked for more details. Perkins padded in quietly, carrying a tray with a silver coffeepot and cups of fine china. He placed it on a sideboard and just as quietly disappeared.

"So, circumstances led you to become a rustler against your will?" Governor Wallace summed up.

"That's right."

"And you're willing to cooperate with us in shutting down this gang in return for—what?"

"Governor, I've read that you offered William Bonney and some others amnesty, and I'd like you to make that same offer to me."

Wallace leaned forward in his high-backed leather chair and, elbows braced on chair arms, made a tent with his extended fingers in front of his face. Cam became uneasy in the silence. The room dimmed as twilight approached. Perkins crept in, lighting the gas lamps around the office, then easing the door closed behind him.

Would the governor grant his request? Or would he summon the state police and have him jailed? Was this a foolish idea, doomed to fail? Cam's palms became damp, and he began to fidget in his chair.

"Mr. Stone." Wallace finally spoke, fixing Cam with a cold, glaring look. "You strike me as brash, selfish young man who has no real regard for anyone or anything but your own venal pleasures. You've taken advantage of your father's largess to pursue a life of wine, women, and song, with never a thought to the consequences of your actions or their effect on your family."

Cam swallowed, nodded assent, but said nothing.

"But it took courage for you to come here and talk to me. You confessed the error of your ways and professed your intent to change. These are the actions of a man, not a criminal. I believe you to be a repentant young man, deserving of a second chance."

Cam's face brightened, and he leaned forward in his chair. "Thank you, sir."

"I'll meet with my attorney general and strike an agreement for your amnesty."

"Thank you, sir."

"Wait. There's more. I'll send a deputy U.S. Marshal to Lincoln to work with Sheriff Garrett, but his identity shall remain undisclosed for the time being. You will return to your gang as if nothing has transpired. You will be watched, and when the time is right, your gang will be rounded up and brought to account. The attorney general will see to it that your association with the gang never becomes a matter of public record, and you will go free."

"Do you mean I'll act as a spy?"

"I do." Wallace paused. "Can you manage it?"

"But what if I become known later?"

"Your amnesty decree, signed by me, sealed and held by the courts, would have to be opened and released to the public. I doubt it will ever come to that. That Sheriff Garrett down there is a man to be reckoned with, and, as I understand it"—Wallace chuckled grimly—"a certain class of men are fleeing Lincoln County like rats from a sinking ship."

Chapter Twenty-nine

The late-afternoon sun felt good on his back as Cam sat by the fire drinking coffee. Pickett, Doc, and Hub rode into camp, with them a tall, one-eyed man called Bob and his pard, a little man called Chunk, who sometimes rode with Pickett. Cam stood and walked to where his rifle leaned against a rock. He was outnumbered, and if the men he'd come to know lined up against him, he'd not see the sunset this day.

"Howdy, boys."

"So, the prodigal son is back." Doc nodded.

"How was them gals in Mesilla?" Hub grinned.

Pickett glowered. "I told you not to leave camp!"

One-eyed Bob and Chunk watched silently, hands on pistol butts.

"You never said any such thing," Cam answered.

"You calling me a liar? No man calls me a liar and gets away with it."

Cam, his eyes fixed on Pickett's, tossed his empty coffee cup aside and calmly picked up the rifle. "That boy you buffaloed back in Tascosa might've backed water, but he ain't here. The man you're facing right now's going to take a lot of killing, so, whenever you're ready . . ." Cam eared back the hammer on the rifle and raised the muzzle to Pickett's belt buckle. ". . . Start the music."

"I'll take him, Boss," Bob offered. For the first time Cam noticed the man's clenched jaw; it looked as if it was hurting him. He spoke through gritted teeth. Somewhere, somebody had broken the fellow's jaw, and it had not set properly.

"Stand easy, you," Doc said, drawing and cocking his pistol and with an outstretched arm aiming at Bob's good eye, the muzzle less than a foot from the man's face. "This ain't your fight." His finger tightened on the trigger.

Silence fell over the camp. There was a hard glint in Cam's eyes no man had seen before. Not anger, not fear, but a cold, deliberate remoteness.

"Boys, I don't want no part of this," Hub said, taking a step backward.

"I reckon he's called your hand, Pickett," Doc said, his eyes never leaving Bob's face. "Are you going to ante up, or are you gonna fold?"

Pickett's hand hovered over the pistol at his side,

paused, and began to shake. This was not what he'd wanted. Things had gotten out of hand. He'd have some of the boys take care of Cam Stone later. Not now, not him, for he saw death in Cam's eyes. His gun hand dropped to his side. "We'll call it a draw for now, Stone. Understand you've been pulling your weight pretty good, and maybe I've been a little rough on you. Looks like maybe it's the best thing that could have happened. You might make a man yet."

Doc flipped the barrel of his pistol upward, eased down the hammer with his thumb, and holstered his pistol.

"It don't end here, Doc," Bob growled through his clenched jaw.

"That's right," Chunk threw in. "We don't hold with what you done."

"Now?" Doc offered, as Hub came forward to side with his friend.

Two-on-two odds were not the kind Bob favored. "Later, I reckon."

"Sure, boys, there's time enough later for both of you and me to finish this," Doc said.

Cutting his eyes away from Cam, Pickett said, "Here's what's doing. There's a good-sized herd we've been scouting. Best time to hit 'em is when they circle up after a morning on the trail to shuck saddles and change horses. Only the guards will be mounted, and then the cook'll call the drovers to eat dinner. We'll go in shooting. Bob, while we run off the herd, you take care of the horse wrangler and run off the cavvy. They'll not come after us if all their horses are scattered and they're afoot. Any questions?"

"Are we taking the herd to the usual place?"

"That's right. And when we're done with that," he said to Cam, "you're going to pay for what you've done. Don't you forget."

"I'll be waiting."

In that moment everyone present understood that the man they had regarded as their leader, a man everybody feared and nobody would cross, was buffaloed.

Later, Cam spoke quietly to Doc. "*Amigo,* thanks for siding with me. I owe you for that."

"A few weeks back I wouldn't have give a hoot in hell about you," Doc said. "But, youngster, you've come a ways."

"Doc, this is the first time in my life I've done something on my own, stood up and faced my trouble instead of running. It gives a man a good feeling," Cam said.

"You're bound to make big tracks in the Territory one of these days, and I'll not see you shot down by the likes of them."

"Why do you stay, Doc? You're not the same as these boys. They have nothing good in them. You do."

Doc pulled out a flask. "See this?" He took a drink. "Took my life from me, and I let it. But"—he put the small bottle back into his vest pocket—"every once in a while I remember what I once was." He started off but paused. "Just not very often, I'm afraid. You need to get out while you can, Cam." He went to check on the horses.

Bad blood became a silent partner in the camp, and the two factions kept apart. Cam, Doc, and Hub decided to stand watches in case Bob tried anything during the night.

Cam passed a tense and restless night. If the men found out he spied for Wallace, it would all be over in a minute. He had little to report so far, but he kept his eyes open in case he heard more about Dunn or saw the man called Stillwell. A few of his questions had drawn raised eyebrows, so Cam knew it was best leave it, to seem like the man the others knew.

He reverted to his sullen ways, catching a glance from Doc occasionally that showed he didn't believe the act for one minute.

Chapter Thirty

David came out to the gathered herd in the light, one-horse runabout. He stopped where Tilman and Juan Javier watched from the saddle. "Did you get the two new hands?"

"Yes, we got 'em," Tilman answered.

"Well, how are things shaping up?"

"Óscar Montoya, one of Santiago's nephews, signed on as our horse wrangler, and we put together a cavvy of thirty horses." Tilman consulted notes in his tally book. "We've got enough for the boys to change out twice a day and some night horses as well."

David nodded. "Good."

"Butter and Neala will take care of the chuck wagon. We've got four mules, and that suits Butter. Catherine and Esperanza will be on horses, and both insist on wearing pants and riding astraddle."

"God knows, we'll be the talk of the county," David grunted.

Tilman didn't comment. He knew better than to argue with Catherine when she made her mind up. "Now, besides you and me, Juan Javier and Krell, Paco and Ignacio Mascarenas, Augusto Olguin and George Rogers signed on as drovers. When we start out, Juan Javier will ride point and keep us on course. Rogers and the Mascarenas brothers will ride drag. We'll depend on them to keep us at the right speed. They'll keep the corners."

"What's that?" Juan Javier asked.

"They keep the stronger cattle moving and out of the way of the weaker stock. They also make sure the back of the herd doesn't spread out any wider than the swing—by that I mean that part of the herd between the leaders and the drag. You don't want 'em overheated."

"I see."

"Now, Juan Javier will keep the swing from getting too long. I figure it'll do if we keep 'em about a quarter of a mile long," Tilman said. "The swing had best be about fifty or sixty feet wide, and we'll squeeze 'em down when we need to, but never less than ten feet across. If we get gaps, the cattle will start running to fill them. That's just the way of 'em. We'll rotate everybody's job except Juan Javier's. He'll keep point all the way."

Juan Javier spoke up. "We've worked out hand signals—well, hat signals. I'll wave my hat in the direction we'll move."

"We'll stop at about eleven o'clock to graze the herd, change out horses, and feed the boys," Tilman said. "When the cattle start to lie down, we'll know they've grazed long enough, and we'll move along."

"How about stopping at night?" David asked.

"Well, we want to hold up before sundown and at a place where there's water. We'll put 'em in a circle. For the first day or so we'll double the guard—half of us for the first part of the night, the rest for the second part. Nobody takes his boots off. We can ease off of that if they look like they're settling down to the trail. After that, night guard will be two men standing watches of two hours and some. The boys know that at night they'll ride around the herd facing each other. That way, they'll pass each other twice in one complete circle around the herd."

"Sounds like you've got a good handle on things," David said.

"One more thing," Tilman said. "Rogers wasn't too sure about the women coming along—he calls 'em 'janes'—but I think he'll be all right with it. I've told the boys there'll be no whiskey, no cards, no fighting among themselves, and, since we've got the ladies along, no cussing."

"Maybe we'd better tell the ladies about those rules too!" David laughed.

"We'll finish the branding today, so we can start 'em moving about daylight tomorrow," Tilman said.

"How many have we got?" David asked.

"Augusto and Juan Javier agree on six hundred fifty-four steers and cows."

"Any calves?"

"Well, you don't want calves on a drive."

"I see."

Chapter Thirty-one

The herd halted at noon so hungry cowboys could change horses and wolf down a dinner of fried beef, beans, and sourdough biscuits. The cattle were grazing on the tall grama grass. James, sleeves rolled up and wearing an apron, was washing and drying the tin plates and spoons and repacking the chuck wagon, complaining that he'd signed on as a drover, not a cook's helper.

"You ladies want to walk upstream of the herd to that nice stand of cottonwood we just passed and clean up a bit? It seems like weeks instead of days since I washed my hair." Esperanza lifted her long hair, held back in a loose snood. "Cattle herding is dusty work."

"Do you think you'll be okay?" David walked his horse near Esperanza and drew rein, fatigue making new lines in his face. The trip had not been difficult, but for a man with a recent wound still not completely healed, travel took its toll.

"We'll be fine, *querido.*"

"Watch out," James cautioned. "Take a gun. Might be a bear out there. Maybe even a panther."

"Yes, nephew. I'll take my rifle in case there's a mean turtle or angry crow down by the stream."

"Aw," James moaned, "you know what I mean."

"We'll be fine, David." Catherine joined Esperanza, followed by Neala.

"I'll make some sourdough doughnuts for tomorrow," Neala said, winking at James. She turned to Esperanza as James went back to work. "He thinks they're very good."

"James isn't the only one," David agreed as he turned his horse back to rejoin the other men. "Be careful, and yell if you need us."

It was cool under the big cottonwoods, and the women were glad to have a moment of rest from the drive. They shucked off their dusty boots and stockings, pulling their riding skirts up to their knees, and rested their tired feet in the cold, clear water. The cottonwood branches filtered the noonday sun, making a quietly peaceful setting broken only by Catherine, Neala, and Esperanza's soft chatter as they took turns washing each other's hair and shaking their locks out to dry in the sun.

"What a nice afternoon," Neala observed. "I like traveling with Mr. Pegram, but the drive gets very tiring, and it feels so good to have clean hair again."

"You're right. And look at us—Catherine with red

hair, and you, Neala, with long blond hair. Such a contrast to my black hair," Esperanza said. "Unfortunately, with gray coming all too soon for me—sons and daughters do that to a mother."

A companionable silence filled the space as the three women enjoyed the moment, each one lost in thought.

"Neala? How are you adjusting to being a wife? You and Butter seem to care so much for each other." Catherine stretched, the sun warming her face. "I am so glad Butter found someone. He offered Tilman a helping hand when Tilman didn't know how to ask for one. Butter helped change the way Tilman sees his place in life."

"Yes, Mr. Pegram is a very special man and the answer to my prayers. I love my brother, but I didn't want to spend my days being his old-maid guest and housekeeper." Neala hesitated. "My brother, now, he is a good man who needs a woman to look after him, but I don't know if the woman's been born who can put up with him. He's so stubborn. I pretended not to hear when he got ornery, but I feel sorry for the woman who agrees to walk down the aisle with him."

Esperanza dipped a galvanized camp bucket into the cold stream to fill it. "Isn't this a beautiful place?" She passed the bucket to Neala. "I had no brothers or sisters, so in the way of the old Spanish, I inherited Rocas Duras. David has managed it well. I don't think I could have done it by myself."

Catherine agreed. "I took care of our place in Colorado before I married Tilman, but everything came harder for me than if I had been a man. Many of the businesses in town forget that women have to be in charge of the land when their menfolk are gone hunting, or to war, or fall ill or die. Some trusted me, but others acted as if I had no brain at all in my head."

"Look at us," Esperanza said. "Me, with grandchildren. Catherine with your son nearing the threshold of his young manhood. And Neala, just married. What a picture we must make."

They weren't the only ones to see the charming tableau. Bob and Chunk had ridden ahead of Pickett's gang, in close pursuit of the herd. They were to scout out the number of drovers riding with Stone, report back to Pickett, and then the gang would hit the herd. Bob's jaw still ached from where Tilman Wagner had broken it weeks before.

"Pass me that bottle, Bob." Chunk looked down the hill at the women below. "Have you ever seen such pretty hair on three women?"

"What do you want to do, Chunk?" Bob squinted with his one good eye, already having taken several long swallows of whiskey to ease the constant throbbing in his jaw. "I want to get even with that black-haired Señora Stone. I been dreaming about her for a long time now."

"I bet they'd like to know a couple of fellers like us." Chunk slapped his thigh in anticipation. He smiled, a gap in his front teeth showing the results of a saloon fight in Mesilla a few years back. He paused. "You know what, Bob?"

"No. What, Chunk?"

"I bet ol' Pick would really like us if we brought him one of them women to get even with Stone and his men. Might use her to make a deal with the old man."

The two men looked at each other and then shook hands. A chance to get on Pickett's good side would be helpful. He'd not been smiling much lately, and when Pickett was unhappy, everybody was unhappy. Bob and Chunk stumbled to their horses, mounted, and headed down the steep hill, threading among the trees, their horses causing rocks to slide before them.

Catherine was combing her hair, enjoying the feel of the sun on her face, when she heard the sound of loose rocks clattering into the stream. "Shh!" She motioned to the other women to be still as she listened for the noise again. Esperanza slowly stood and stepped into the shadow behind a large cottonwood trunk.

Suddenly two men on horses rode into view on the other side of the stream.

"Howdy, ladies. You wait right there," Bob called as he and Chunk rode into the water.

"What are two pretty ladies like you doing out here?" Chunk asked. Then he paused and said, "Hey, where's the third 'un?"

A shot banged from behind the tree, and Chunk's hat flew from his head. "Hoo-ah!" he yelped in surprise, pulling his head close to his shoulders and reining to a stop midstream. "You almost shot my ear off!"

"Clear out now if you value your worthless lives!" Esperanza came out from behind the tree, her rifle in her hands. "I know who you are. You threatened me once before. Now, I mean business. I am tired, and I won't hesitate to shoot two worthless excuses for men." Esperanza shouldered the rifle and aimed it, but the men whirled their horses around and headed back for the hill as fast as they could. The three ladies heard the wounded man cursing a blue streak as held his bandana to a bloody ear.

"Catherine!" Tilman raced from the nearby camp, his horse sliding to a dusty stop. "What happened?" He saw a calm Esperanza standing there, a cloud of gun smoke drifting lazily, thinning in the still air.

"Oh, Tilman." Catherine looked at her husband. "You have quite a sister-in-law. Wouldn't you say so, Neala?"

"She's quite a shot, is she not?" Neala laughed aloud, a clear, tinkling laugh that turned into a chortle as the adrenaline hit. "I think she gets two of my doughnuts in the morning. Do you agree, Catherine?"

Tilman shook his head as the three women ignored him, walking off arm in arm back to the camp, leaving him to follow. *Women.* He'd never understand them if he lived to be a hundred. Later, he'd find out from Catherine what had happened. Whatever it was, the women didn't want to talk just now, and he wasn't about to start anything. He could wait. He'd learned that much. Catherine would talk when she was ready.

Evening found the three women and the men enjoying an unexpected treat. Catherine had whipped up some hoecakes with some of the cornmeal and then sliced and fried a chunk of smoked bacon that had been hanging in the back of the chuck wagon. Using coffee and drippings, she'd also put together some red-eye gravy.

"I swear, Catherine, I don't know where you learned to cook. I never saw our mother in the kitchen when we were small. Did she change after I left?" David licked his fingers, the gravy making a feast of the hoecakes and bacon.

"No, brother of mine. Our mother never entered the kitchen except to tell somebody what she wanted to eat. But"—Catherine paused—"I had a fine teacher when I first moved to Colorado. One of the neighbors came over, and when she saw that my gravy was so solid, it jiggled, she took pity on me and taught me all she knew. She still wins awards at the fairs every year."

Tilman got up and stretched his legs. "Think I'll take a look at the night hawks. The cattle seem restless tonight. Could be a there's a panther out there. Juan Javier, do you want to take the other side?" The two men rode into the night as the fire burned down to embers. The night guards reassured them that nothing was amiss, so the two were soon back in camp.

Chapter Thirty-two

The following day the rustlers hit them.

They'd come maybe five miles since daylight over pretty rough up-and-down country. The horses showed wear, and the hungry men all welcomed Juan Javier's hat signal to circle the herd.

Tilman, on drag all morning, rode up to tell George and Augusto, "You've been riding swing, so you'll take first guard while the rest of us eat, and then we'll spell you."

"Don't you all dally." George grinned. "I got a whiff of that tall woman's cooking just now, and my stomach's been asking me if my throat's been cut."

Tilman left his horse with the cavvy and walked across the camp to where the hands began lining up for the women to dish out the chuck. David, holding his horse at the edge of the camp, announced to all, "You've got a real treat. We're having Pennsylvania shoo-fly pie today!"

Suddenly a fusillade of shots and yells rang out, and Tilman saw the herd bolt straight for the camp. "Get the women up in those trees!" he yelled while running to gather up James and send him scrambling up an oak tree. Out of the corner of his eye, he saw David's pitching horse, back bowed up and crow-hopping through the camp, the man losing his seat and falling to the ground, landing hard. He did not see Esperanza rush to David's side and drag him to shelter in a rock cleft. The other men desperately ran for the closest trees with low limbs. Tilman pushed Catherine into the same massive oak where James perched fearfully before climbing up beside her and wrapping his arms around her and James. He'd lost sight of Butter and Neala.

The herd thundered through the camp, all horns and hooves and bellowing steers raising a thick cloud of dust. The force of the rush was so great, the chuck wagon tipped over onto one side, setting the fly tent flapping and further spooking the steers. Dimly seen through the dust behind the steers came several riders, their faces hidden behind bandanas under hats pulled down low, shouting and firing pistols into the air.

They vanished almost as suddenly as they had come, rumbling back down the trail the herd had come up that morning. After the sudden violence, silence lay over the camp, the dust settling.

Men dropped from nearby trees and stared in wonder at the wreckage of the camp. The fire had been scattered and the coffeepot and washtubs flattened by hooves. Tilman helped Catherine and James down.

Esperanza stood by a pile of rocks, and Tilman called to her, "Is David all right?"

"His wound is bleeding again," she answered.

"I've lost another herd to those damned rustlers!" David protested.

"Hush," Esperanza chided. "Be still."

"I'll go help," Catherine said, rushing to where David sat, his shoulders sagging in defeat, one hand holding his side.

"Butter!" Tilman called. "Neala?"

"Here we are!" Butter answered from behind the root mass of a fallen pine.

"Dirty but all in one piece," Neala said. "Mr. Pegram saved my life," she added in wonderment. "Did you see? He picked me up and carried me behind that tree! Running, he was!" She planted a big kiss on Butter's dusty cheek.

"Somebody go check on the boys who were on guard. I don't see 'em, and I'm afraid they might be done for."

"How about a little help here?" George Rogers called, his voice tight with pain, from the wreckage that had been the edge of the camp. The drover leaned on Juan Javier's shoulder, his face livid, one bootless and bloody foot held off the ground.

"They got Augusto. He's over there." Juan Javier pointed with his chin. "Óscar is all right, just sitting by him. George's foot doesn't look too good. Bullet messed it up pretty bad."

"James, get the fire going again, and rustle up some pots. We need hot water to clean up Mr. Rogers and your Uncle David."

"Yes, sir," James answered.

Tilman surveyed the wreckage. David was right. They'd lost the herd. He had failed. He'd let his guard down. Things had been going well, and they'd caught him by surprise.

Chapter Thirty-three

John Chisum sat his horse and watched as his cowboys worked the wooded hills and brushy draws to drive foxy old cows and their wild, unbranded calves out of hiding and start them drifting down toward the place where the small herd was gathered. Chisum's range had long been a favorite of rustlers, but he'd had some luck at holding them at bay ever since he started paying his men gun wages of four dollars a day. Sure, an ordinary cowboy of eighteen or nineteen was eager to work, and you could count on him to ride for the brand for a dollar a day and found. Nevertheless, you couldn't ask him to risk his life going up against cattle rustlers. Most of Chisum's riders were in their mid- to late twenties with a hard edge to them. What they lacked in cow smarts they more than made up for in their skills with a six-gun or a rifle. Pickings were pretty slim on the quarter of the range they were working, so Chisum decided that after today, he'd shift his men around to the northeast.

"Mr. Chisum!" A shout came across the rolling prairie. "Come look here!" One of the boys, Jas Morgan, stood in his stirrups, waving his hat to get Chisum's attention.

The hard-eyed old rancher spurred his mount and soon reined up alongside the cowboy.

"What in the world?" From the crest of a low hill, Chisum saw on the flats below a man lying on the ground, two women kneeling beside him, and several men standing around a chuck wagon turned on its side in a ruined camp. Not a horse or cow was in sight. The folks below looked to be stranded.

"Boss, unless rustlers have taken to bringing women and a chuck wagon on the trail, I'd say that's some outfit lost everything in a stampede."

"Let's get down there and see." Chisum spurred his horse and started down the hill. As he got closer, a tall man stepped out to greet him, one hand resting on the six-gun at his side. "Hold your fire. I mean no harm."

"Mr. Chisum, isn't it?" the tall man said. "It's been a while."

"Do I know you?" Chisum leaned down for a closer look at Tilman.

"You were putting together a herd a few years back, and I was fixin' to throw in with my small herd. Things didn't work out."

"Indian trouble, as I recall."

"That's right. Killed my wife."

"You're Wagner? Heard you went off on a tear. Cleaned up some hard cases out around the South Llano River country."

"I did for a fact."

"What's all this?" Chisum asked. "And who's that laying yonder—is that David Stone?" He swung down, and he and Tilman went to look at David's condition. Jas and another cowboy used their horses and lariats for pulling, and, with the help of the other men pushing, the chuck wagon was set upright again with little real damage. Flour and green coffee beans spilled from the chuck box lay in heaps on the ground, and several bedrolls had gone adrift as well. The water barrel had shattered, reduced to broken staves and bent hoops.

To Butter's way of thinking, it appeared a good thing that the wagon fell onto its left side, crushing the water barrel instead of the coffee grinder mounted on its right side. He'd perish without fresh ground coffee. It was too bad about the coffeepot, but a man could always boil coffee in any kind of pot.

A Dutch oven, frying pan, and several tin plates and cups were scattered on the ground from the open boot. The short man and his tall, blond wife busied themselves setting the wagon back in order.

Tilman explained. "They hit us about the time we'd circled the herd and the boys were gathered at the chuck wagon for dinner. Ran off our horses, took the herd. Augusto Olguin and George Rogers were circling the herd. The rustlers killed Augusto and shot George in the foot. David took a tumble from his horse, and a wound he'd gotten earlier reopened."

"They left us here for the coyotes to have." Juan Javier joined the two men, acknowledging Chisum. "Mr. Chisum. Good thing you found us."

"I'll send Jas to get some horses, and if you tell me what else you need, I'll try to get it for you." Chisum motioned to David. "That's a good man. He's always tried to be fair about things, and in this Territory, that's a rare trait."

"Don't talk about me as if I were dead!" David shouted, brushing away Catherine's attempts to comfort him. "Leave me be, sister. I'm just a little shaken up. I'll be fine." He tried to rise, but with a sharp intake of breath he paled, lying back down as the hole in his side began to ooze blood again.

"Be still, *querido*." Esperanza kneeled beside him and spoke with a honeyed voice that nonetheless brooked no nonsense.

"I've an idea," David said weakly. "I'll do just that."

The sun was midway down the afternoon sky when Jas returned, driving a dozen horses. One of Chisum's men took a pick and a shovel to help Óscar wrap Augusto Olguin in a blanket and lower him into a grave. The men removed their hats, and Butter said a few words after they shoveled earth over the *vaquero*. Óscar fashioned a crude cross and vowed to come back with a better marker for the grave of his friend. The men piled rocks over the mounded dirt of the grave.

Jas also brought a packhorse with two small kegs of drinking water. Neala and Butter shooed Catherine and Esperanza away while they fried bacon and warmed leftover biscuits in sizzling bacon grease. A Dutch oven full of beans simmered under a pile of hot coals. Butter scooped ground coffee by the handful into a tin pot of water and hung it from a tripod over the fire to boil. "The eggs got broke," Butter apologized, "so I can't settle the grinds out."

Neala sprinkled sugar and cinnamon on the hot sourdough biscuits, and the men ate as they discussed what to do next.

Chisum's cowboys, hard cases who lived by the gun, were unaccustomed to women in a cow camp. Where most working cowboys might have a six-gun they couldn't hit anything with, or an old Henry rifle or a shotgun tucked inside their blanket rolls in the possum belly slung beneath the chuck wagon, these men wore well-kept weapons and knew how to use them. Still, they showed their best manners and were quick with praise for the cooks. With the hearty appetites of strong young men who worked out of doors, they cleaned their tin plates, sopping up bean juice with biscuits. Their scraped plates and forks were dumped into boiling water in one of the washtubs that Tilman had pried open and bent back into usable shape. With waves and repeated thank-you's the men tightened saddle cinches, mounted, and rode off to rejoin their outfit.

Chisum made sure that David and his party took what he had in the way of extras. "Keep an eye out. The fellows hitting us may be Los Diablos, but we haven't been able to catch anyone yet, so I can't say for sure." He paused. "One of my boys thinks a Texan by the name of Pickett is calling the shots. He'd better hope the sheriff gets him before my boys do, for we've got new rope that needs stretching." He mounted his horse and touched his hat to the ladies.

Tilman watched as the rancher rode off to rejoin his men. He turned to survey the camp. There was no question what came next. Get it done.

Chapter Thirty-four

"It's pretty clear that David and George both need to get to a doctor, so I say we send them off in the back of the chuck wagon," Tilman said in the quiet that followed. "The ladies can go back with them too, and then," he said, his voice taking on a hard edge, "we're going to get that herd."

"And the men who took it," Juan Javier said.

"Dad, I want to stay with you." James stood as tall as he could, holding the little Belgian-made .22 rifle that he'd pulled from the chuck wagon. "I can ride and shoot pretty good, and you need me more than Mom does."

Catherine put a hand on James' shoulder. "I think I need you to stay with me."

"She's right, son." The boy was too young for this kind of work.

David lay on a pallet in the back of the wagon, his head

in Esperanza's lap. George Rogers sat beside David, his painfully aching and heavily bandaged foot elevated on his bedroll. Neala turned the heavy, springless wagon back for Rocas Duras, trying to avoid rocks and ruts in the road, while Catherine sat on the seat beside her with a rifle across her lap. James, riding proudly on one of Chisum's sure-footed cow ponies, followed the wagon.

Tilman, Butter, Juan Javier, Walter Krell, Óscar Montoya, and the Mascarenas brothers, Paco and Nacho, set a fast pace across the rolling hills, for even a blind man could have followed the trail left by the herd. The day had turned hot and still under harsh, brittle sunlight, with not a breath of air stirring. The men felt a sense of unease.

The sun rode low in the hazy afternoon sky, almost touching the dark rim of mountains to the west. Tilman couldn't shake the uneasy feeling. Something was amiss, and he kept looking back over his shoulder.

"Tilman, what's got you spooked?" Butter rode by his side.

"I could swear somebody's watching us."

"Want me to circle around and check our back trail?"

"No, let's keep on."

The evening sky was darkening when the men made a dry camp with no fire. Supper was a quick meal of corn dodgers washed down with water from canteens.

"No salt?" Butter complained. "What kind of sorry outfit have I signed on with?"

"Neala's cooking has spoiled you for roughing it," Tilman said.

"This is odd," Juan Javier said to Krell. "We've been riding southeast toward Fort Stanton. Where do you think they're driving that herd?"

"Is Rustler's Cave down that way, maybe?" Krell asked. "The place people talked about in the Lincoln County War?" At Juan Javier's nod, Krell continued. "Mr. Wagner, we have an idea."

"Where'd Wagner go?" Juan Javier asked, looking around.

"Ow. Take it easy, Dad." James sheepishly came out from a clump of scrubby mountain cedars, his pony plodding along behind. Tilman walked beside James, clearly exasperated with his young son.

"You'd better talk fast, young man." Tilman didn't know whether to hug his son or paddle him. "What is your mother going to think?"

"She knows where I am. She didn't want me to come, but I told her it was time she let me be a man," James declared.

Tilman looked at the other men, shaking his head. "What can I do? It's too late to send him back."

"The man is ready to come out of the boy." Paco grinned, elbowing Nacho in the side. "See how he stands by his father?"

Tilman fixed James with a hard stare. "You'll do what I say?"

"Yes, sir, Dad, sir. Oh, gee." James hugged Tilman and then remembered where he was and stood straight. "I have to see to my horse."

"He'll do, Tilman." Butter shook out a blanket to turn in. "Wonder where he got it from."

Well before daylight, the men saddled up and headed out into the darkness. Yesterday had been hot, the air still yet filled with the silence that builds before a storm on the plains. Thunder rumbled in the distance, and lightning flashes lit huge cloud masses like the Chinese lanterns Esperanza had strung for the party. Jagged bolts flashed, taking giant steps across the predawn horizon. James was wide awake, full of excitement as he guided his horse behind Tilman's.

"My finger hurts," Butter complained. "Bet it's gonna rain."

"Which finger is that?" Krell asked.

"My right-hand trigger finger."

"You don't have one, so how can it hurt?"

"Just 'cause I got it shot off in a tussle down near the border don't mean it can't hurt! Ain't you never heard folks missing a leg say it itches?"

Óscar and the Mascarenas brothers rode in silence, each making the sign of the Cross. They were *vaqueros,* and none had ever shot at a man, but today they rode for the brand against men who had killed and would kill again.

The men were silent, each alone with his thoughts, none sure what lay ahead. Tilman doubted the wisdom of allowing James to ride with them. Too late now to worry. Would they get the herd back? Would anyone be hurt? Maybe even killed? Who could know the outcome of what they were about to do? But each man was sure that, although someone else might be hurt or killed, it would not be himself. None could admit death might be waiting to take him this day.

Tilman alone of the riders could be called a fighting man, experienced in hunting down other men, risking his life while bringing them to justice or killing them. He had been shot and had no illusions about how easy it was for a random bullet to take a life. It was a way of living he thought he'd left behind. Odd, how some things lay just below the surface of a man, barely hidden beneath a civilized veneer but easily brought back into play when needed. His blood still quickened with the sounds of gunfire and bullets singing past him. He spoke a quiet prayer for himself and those who rode with him.

"The usual plan?" Butter spoke in a low voice.

"I reckon," Tilman answered.

"What plan?" Juan Javier asked, his voice tight with stress, afraid he'd missed a strategy session.

"The plan is, there ain't no plan," Butter explained. "Wagner always has to see what's what before he decides what we'll do."

"Oh," Walter Krell said, doubt clear in his tone.

"Works ever' time," Butter said.

"I think I understand why you have only nine fingers now," Juan Javier said.

"Hush, boys, we're getting close. Butter, drop back, and take James with you."

Chapter Thirty-five

Above the men, bright stars defined the dome of the moonless early-morning sky. A light breeze stirred, bringing the smell of wood smoke and coffee across the dark prairie. In the north, stars disappeared behind rising storm clouds. Lightning flashed inside the clouds, followed by muted, distant thunder. Somewhere a steer bawled, spooked by the sounds.

"Hold up," Tilman whispered hoarsely.

Leather creaked as he dismounted. Walter and Juan Javier did the same.

"You two take the horses over that little hill behind us. Tell the others to stay by you and keep the horses quiet. I'm going to take a look at their camp."

"I'm going with you," Juan Javier said.

"Now, look—"

"I'm going," Juan Javier insisted.

Tilman hesitated and then said, "That storm's getting closer, and we don't have time to argue. Let's take off these spurs, and leave your hat here. You stay close behind me."

The earlier breeze gave way to a dead calm. Lightning flashes gave glimpses of their surroundings, but the delayed arrival of the rumbling thunder meant that the approaching storm was yet several miles distant. The lowing of nervous cattle became louder. A sudden cough close by startled Tilman. He turned and motioned for Juan Javier to stay down. The two men eased themselves to the top of a low rise. Peering around a jumble of rocks, they saw the rustlers' camp below them. A man bent to push sticks of dry wood into the coals of a campfire. Another man took a coffeepot from the coals, stood, and poured himself a cup of the steaming liquid. He drank deeply. The dry wood caught and blazed, and in the firelight Tilman recognized the man. Fields!

"How's a man supposed to get any sleep around here?" a third man complained, stepping into the light. "You could wake the dead with that cough."

Fields struggled to regain his breath, coughed again, drew a medicine bottle from his shirt pocket, and drank from it. "This laudanum will likely kill me before my lungs give out," he said, "but I aim to kill you first, Stone."

A sharp intake of breath from Juan Javier was answer enough for Tilman's unspoken question. "Is that Cam?" Tilman whispered.

"Yes!"

"Come on. Let's get back where we can talk."

Tilman and Juan Javier rejoined Krell, Butter, and the three drovers. A wide-eyed James had strung a rope and had the horses tied so he could manage them all. Sensing Juan Javier's anger, James tugged at Tilman's sleeve. "What's going on, Dad?" he whispered. "Why is Juan Javier so mad?"

Tilman hushed James.

Juan Javier needed a moment to get himself under control, for he shook with barely suppressed anger. "Cam!" he muttered. "Cam stole from us. My own brother!" Juan Javier's eyes glittered in the flashes of lightning, his words punctuated by thunder. Angrily he paced, muttering Spanish words that Tilman did not know, but he could guess their meaning. Finally the young man settled down.

"What's the layout, Tilman?" Butter asked.

"Three of them up and about, and I saw two more still in their blankets. I figure there's at least one out there keeping watch over the herd."

"Uh-huh," Butter said. "Looks like six or seven of them against the seven of us. I like them odds."

"One of 'em, the one sounds like a lunger, I recognized. Fields, he called himself. I knew him from Texas. He's a killer."

"Fields?" Juan Javier said, "No, his name is Stillwell. He's Franklin Dunn's foreman."

"What? *That* explains a lot! I talked to him for a moment at the dance several weeks ago and knew he worked for Dunn, but I didn't know what he called himself now. He was no good when I knew him, and he's gotten no better since." Tilman paused. "Wonder what Dunn's part in this is? Oh, well, no matter now. We're going to take back that herd, and some folks will answer the hard questions later."

A sudden cold wind gusted, sending a chill through the men. Tilman looked at the sky and said, "With this storm blowing in, they'll have their hands full keeping the cattle bunched. Let's get ready, and when it breaks, we'll ride in shooting, take 'em by surprise."

"Cam is mine," Juan Javier growled. His hands balled into fists as he tried to restrain a mixture of anger and hurt. *Cam!* His own brother!

Butter stepped over to stand by Juan Javier. "Listen, son. I don't begin to know the whole story here, but just you remember that it would kill your mother if she thought you had anything to do with Cam's being harmed. Mothers can be strange people when it comes to their children. For one of their own to go against others in the family—right or wrong, makes no difference—it hurts bad. Nothing good ever comes when family goes against family."

"Cam didn't think of that."

"Makes no never-mind. *You* know better. Think of that. Goes back to Cain and Abel, if you're a Bible-reading man. If not, call it plain common sense."

Walter came to Juan Javier's side. "Think of your sisters. This could hurt them badly," Walter continued. "If Cam's gone bad, the law'll take care of him. But for now we've got us a battle to fight." Krell's Adam's apple bobbed, but he nodded his head, game if not eager.

"Check your sidearms," Butter suggested, "and put a shell under the hammer. You'll need all six when the ball opens."

"I don't have a sidearm," Krell said. "I've got my daddy's shotgun, and that will have to do."

"James, you stay here. I'll be back for you." Tilman turned to give James a quick hug. He knew this night would strengthen his son. Life could be hard, and James lived in a rough time, but he had the makings to become a fine man.

"Yes, sir," James answered. "But Mom said for me to tell you to be careful."

Within a few minutes the mounted men neared the camp, guns drawn, breath coming short and quick with nervous anticipation. The first drops of rain *plakked* into the dry ground around them. A chilly wind gusted, then roared over them; lightning and thunder became almost continuous. The first line of heavy rain approached to engulf the camp.

"Heavy dew a-comin'," Butter whispered. "Turn your collars up."

A blast of pea-sized hail came rattling in, stinging men and horses.

"Now!" Tilman yelled, spurring forward as the others followed.

Chapter Thirty-six

The battle quickly became a nightmarish confusion of gunfire in the rain and darkness, amid screaming horses, shouting men, thunder and lightning, and the rumble of stampeding cattle. Above all the sounds Tilman heard the bloodcurdling yip and howl of Butter's Rebel yell. Tilman's first shot caught one man sitting up in his blankets, gun in hand, the slug knocking the man flat. Krell, who had never used a gun from the saddle, fired a shotgun blast at another rustler, the load of shot missing the man by yards but exploding the fire into a dazzling red spray of coals and shredding the coffeepot, releasing a thick cloud of steam into the air.

"What's this?" Pickett rode in from the other side of the campfire. He'd fallen asleep in the saddle while on watch, only to be jolted awake by the riders invading the camp. Cursing angrily, he circled, trying to come in behind Tilman and his men. Bob and Chunk and the other men scrambled for their horses, bringing their guns into play.

Stillwell, struggling to control his plunging horse and get a saddle onto him, snapped off a shot that killed Juan Javier's horse. As the animal collapsed and slid into the camp, Juan Javier simply stepped from the saddle to hit the ground running straight for a startled Cam. The other riders swept through the camp and disappeared into the darkness.

In the suddenness of the fighting, Cam had no idea who the attackers could be, but he gasped, "Juanito!" when a flash of lightning showed the man bearing down on him with a pistol to be his brother.

"Juanito! Wait! It's not how it looks!" The sudden onslaught overwhelmed Cam. Time seemed to slow to a crawl. He saw everything with a clarity he had never experienced; he felt as if he were a spectator in the battle unfolding around him. Behind Juan Javier, Cam saw Chunk at the edge of the camp, fighting to control a gun-spooked horse, draw his pistol and aim at Juan Javier.

"Look out!" Cam shouted, pointing his own pistol at the rustler. Cam's words were lost in the noise of battle, unheard by Juan Javier, who only saw his brother pointing a pistol at him.

Juan Javier raised his pistol, cocking the hammer back, aiming it at Cam.

Chunk's pistol flared with fire, the smoke whipped

away by the wind, the sound no more than a muffled *pop* lost in the battle sounds. The bullet struck Juan Javier, and he collapsed like a puppet without strings.

"Damn you!" Cam screamed as his pistol roared. It was a snap shot at a moving target aboard a plunging horse in semidarkness, but the lead slug took the man through the forehead, killing him before his body left the horse to slam into the dirt beside Juan Javier.

Cam knelt by his fallen brother, the rain spreading a pool of blood across the hard-packed ground. "Juanito, no, don't die!" He turned his brother over, embracing him while using his bandana to staunch the flow of blood from the wound in his back.

"I saw . . ." Juan Javier muttered.

"You don't know what you saw," Cam pleaded. "Chunk had you under his gun. This isn't how it looks. I'm on your side."

Juan Javier groaned as the pain came.

"Brother, don't die!"

"I meant to kill you, Cam," Juan Javier gasped, looking at the dead rustler lying beside him.

"You wouldn't have pulled the trigger." Cam looked for help. There was none. The others had vanished as the battle, taking on a life of its own, moved across the prairie. "Be quiet, and save your breath. I have to get you to a doctor." Juan Javier appeared to be fading fast. "Can you help me get you onto a horse?"

"*Sí, mi hermano.* I can," he said weakly. Juan Javier fainted in Cam's arms.

Cam checked the bandana. It was soaked. His eyes

went to Chunk's bandana. He ripped it off the dead man, jamming it over Juan Javier's wound. Chunk's horse stood nearby, reins dangling. Cam caught the horse and gathered up his brother's limp body. He pushed Juan Javier into the saddle and climbed up behind him. With luck, they could reach Fort Stanton by morning. Before it was too late.

The two brothers vanished into the raging storm as Tilman and the others tried to control the storm-crazed herd.

Chapter Thirty-seven

The cattle stampeded, thundering in a tight bunch onto the prairie and into the teeth of the storm, the clash and clatter of their horns rising above the other sounds. Between lightning flashes the morning was unfathomably dark, the wild ride across the prairie a terror to blinded men, unknown ravines, knolls, and gullies becoming hazards to those riding hard after the herd. Balls of lightning rolled across the ground from strikes nearby and charged the air with electricity. A strange glow of Saint Elmo's fire danced across the herd, providing some light for the fearful men.

Butter whipped his horse alongside the herd, racing to help turn them, but he had to pull aside because of the unbearably intense heat given off by the running animals. One of the rustlers, a cowboy in spite of his owl-hoot ways, pushed his pony hard to get to the leaders of the herd and, after several miles, managed to turn them to the right. He pushed them until the leaders caught up with the tail end of the herd, causing them to slow to a walk and then settle into a "mill." As that happened, Tilman watched in amazement from across the herd as the unknown man reined in his hard-breathing pony, produced a flask from his vest pocket, and upended it. Noticing Tilman, the man waved a wordless salute with the flask. He tossed it aside, then turned and rode over a knoll to vanish from sight.

By dawn the fight had ended, and the storm had rained itself out in the far distance, leaving the herd milling in the damp stillness, a few cattle beginning to munch grasses. Butter waved his hat to get Tilman's attention. "Come look here!"

Tilman walked his horse to see what Butter wanted, and Krell joined the two men.

"Would you look at that!" Butter said, pointing at the body of one of the rustlers, a man with a patch over one eye. The man's horse had been struck by lightning, the bridle bit melted in the horse's mouth, silver conchos on the saddle melted, and the shoes knocked off the animal's hooves.

"Who was he?" Krell asked.

"No idea."

"I thought it might be Juan Javier," Tilman said, emptying spent cartridge cases from his pistol and replacing them with fresh loads. "I've not seen him."

"I did," Butter said. "I saw him lying on the ground. Then one of the rustlers put him onto a horse and rode away during the fight. Mighty odd, that was."

"You don't suppose Cam rode off with Juan Javier," Krell wondered. "Juan Javier said his brother was part of this outfit."

"Could be. I didn't see him, though," Tilman said.

"Who's that?" Krell said, pointing at a man wading across a shallow stream.

"A rustler!" Butter said, drawing his pistol.

"Come on," Tilman said, spurring his horse.

The riders surrounded the man on foot. "Hold on. Don't shoot. I ain't armed."

"Fields," Tilman said, "or Stillwell—whatever your name is. So you're the one behind this."

"To hell with you, Wagner," Stillwell spat.

Tilman had no plans to go through with a hanging, but a good scare might make Stillwell talk. "Tie his hands, Krell," Tilman said, taking the coiled rope from his saddle.

He turned to Stillwell. "I aim to hang you—something I should have done a long time ago." Tilman saw a line of cottonwoods by the stream. "Over there, you."

"Now wait a minute, Wagner," Stillwell sputtered. Tilman's reputation around the Texas hill country was well-known. "You can't just hang a man without no trial."

"That's right, but I can sure string up a rustler." Tilman grimly fashioned a hangman's noose and tossed it over a handy limb, looping the end to his saddle horn. He shoved Stillwell under the rope and adjusted the noose around the protesting man's neck. Climbing into the saddle, Tilman backed his horse, taking up slack in the rope until Stillwell balanced on tiptoe.

Stillwell broke into a spasm of coughing and, when that subsided, crying, begging for his life. Tilman backed his horse, almost lifting Stillwell into the air. The man screamed, and water puddled beneath him.

"Wagner," Butter said, nodding toward an approaching rider. It was James.

Tilman looked, took a deep breath, and urged his pony forward. Stillwell collapsed in a sobbing heap of misery. A shaken Walter Krell removed the noose.

"All right, you're not smart enough to put this together," Tilman barked to Stillwell. "Who's behind this?"

"Dunn," Stillwell gasped. "Dunn is crazy for money. Wants Stone's ranch and anybody else's he can take. Cattle, horses, Stone's youngest daughter—he wants it all."

"Beatriz?" Walter stood still. "That good-for-nothing!"

Tilman motioned with a hand for James to hold up where he was. James reined up and watched from a short distance the strange tableau unfolding before him.

"Who else is in on it?"

"Pickett is. He disappeared at the first sign of trouble, though. Probably headed back to Tascosa and his hangout. I saw him leave, and he never looked back. Him and some old gal over there run a card scam and roped young Stone into this. Figgered he'd be a good front."

"Young Stone, you say?" The news would destroy David and Esperanza.

"Who else?" Butter demanded.

"That's all," Stillwell said.

"He's a-sullin' up," Butter said to Tilman, "so let's put that noose back on and hoist him up again and see what he says."

"No!" Stillwell gasped as Butter draped the noose over his head.

"How did Dunn know who was coming and going on the RD?" Tilman asked. "How did he know when the men were away?" His pony backed, and the rope drew tight.

"Wait, wait!" Stillwell cried through gritted teeth.

Tilman slacked the rope.

"There's an old, pensioned-off soldier with an Army forge goes around ranches to shoe horses. Calls himself Sarge. He's on Dunn's payroll. He spied on Stone and let Dunn know the best time to hit the ranch." Stillwell groaned. "Dunn'll kill me if he knows I sold him out."

"Not if I get him first." Tilman smiled grimly.

"Dad? May I come in now?" James called.

At the sound of the boy's voice, a cold anger lifted from Tilman's shoulders. He exhaled, shoulders slumping in tired resignation. There was a time when he'd have gone after Franklin Dunn, never stopping until he had Dunn under his gun. But that was in the past. He didn't hunt men down, not like that, not anymore.

"You all right, pard?" Butter asked.

"Yeah. We'll let the law take this from here." Tilman turned to Paco and Ignacio, motioning to Stillwell and two other rustlers the brothers had rounded up. "Tie these varmints up real good. We don't want them to go anyplace."

The men nodded, glad to have something to do and glad to have the rustlers at bay. Tilman looked for Walter, who seemed to be in shock.

"Walter, you get back to David and let him know about Cam and Juan Javier. That man will heal a lot quicker knowing those two boys are alive and kicking. We'll figure out about Cam when we get home. There's bound to be more to this than what meets the eye. I don't know Cam, but I know his family, and something doesn't ring true."

Krell nodded, wheeled his mount, and took off for the ranch.

Tilman pulled out his tally book and stub pencil. He motioned to Ignacio Mascarenas. "Nacho, take this note to the sheriff in Lincoln. We can wait a day or two for him to come get Stillwell while we pull the herd back together."

"What about this Pickett fellow, Tilman?" Butter watched as Tilman wrote.

"He'll think he's outsmarted us, but I'll let the sheriff know, and he can write to Sheriff Willingham in Tascosa. He's a good man, and he'll take care of things."

"James, you keep an eye on the prisoners until help comes," Tilman said. "Sing out if you think they're trying to get loose."

The rustlers remained securely tied to a stand of scrub oaks in the middle of the cattle, but James took his duties seriously and watched carefully from the saddle a short distance away. He knew that snakes could slither if given a chance, and he intended to do his part to see they had no chance at all. Tilman, Butter, Óscar, and Paco set about rounding up what remained of the herd.

Chapter Thirty-eight

The Rocas Duras was a beehive of activity when Walter wearily slid off his horse. Tom Clark, the post surgeon from Fort Stanton, met him on the steps.

"What are you doing here? Is Mr. Stone worse?"

"Hold up, young man. Mr. Stone is going to be fine. We got his wound cleaned, packed with lint, and wrapped up, and he's resting. I also told him that his boys are safe at the fort."

"Thank you, sir. If you'll excuse me." Walter wanted to know more about Cam and Juan Javier, but he had to take a message to David first. He went inside the house and left the surgeon on his own.

"Mr. Stone?"

Esperanza motioned for Krell to be quiet, but David heard him and called out.

"Esperanza, I'm not going to expire anytime soon, the good Lord willing. Let the boy in for a minute."

David lay captive, surrounded by women. Catherine and Neala were hovering nearby, ready to help in any way. Walter stood still. "It looks more like a quilting bee than a sickroom." He blushed as he spoke.

The women, taking the ill-concealed hint, rose as one to leave the men alone. "You're right, Walter. We'll leave you two men for a little while. Come on, girls. Let's go find something to 'quilt'." An anxious Catherine hesitated at the door.

"Your son is fine, Mrs. Wagner," Walter reassured her. "James makes no demands, and he pulls his own weight. The men like him. He's a fine young man."

"Thank you, Walter. I think you're a fine man yourself, and some woman will be really lucky to marry you one day."

Walter turned as red as the curtains, and David laughed for the first time in days. Life did go on.

"How did you leave Tilman, Butter, and my men?"

"They were fine when I left. Can't say the same for Stillwell and his boys. Tilman threatened to string him up, and I think he would have." Walter paused. "Stillwell believed him as well, because he talked a blue streak. Guess who's behind this whole thing, Mr. Stone?"

"I've got an idea. By any chance is it my newest neighbor, Mr. Franklin Dunn?"

Walter looked surprised. "How did you know?"

"Just an idea I came up with while I was resting in this bed. Seemed too much a coincidence that he moved here and things started to fall apart." David motioned for Walter to help him sit up better. "Any idea where he is now?"

"No, sir. But Mr. Wagner will find him. That much I'm sure of." Walter paused. "Have you heard about Juan Javier? Wasn't Cam out there?"

"Slow down, boy. Juan Javier is going to be fine. The bullet went right through his side, and he's at Fort Stanton with Cam." He stopped and got a drink of water. "Cam saved his life and swears things are not what they seem. We'll have to see." It was quiet. David dozed off, and Walter left the sickroom.

Ignacio found Pat Garret in Lincoln, and the sheriff called out a posse. Within hours the riders set out to help Tilman, arriving at the camp a day later.

Tilman shook hands with Sheriff Garrett. "Appreciate the help, that's for sure."

"Got your note, and I sent one along to Sheriff Willingham. Pickett's days are numbered. You aren't the first to connect him to something like this." Garrett looked around. "Where are Stillwell and his crew?"

"Over there. Other side of the cattle. Seemed like eating dust downwind of the herd was a fitting place for them. Stillwell's been complaining about the flies biting him." Butter joined the two men, Tilman making the introductions.

"Pleasure is mine, Garrett. Heard talk about you from some of the boys. I believe about half of it, and that's likely too much."

"Probably should cut even that by half, and you might be close to the truth of it," Garrett replied humbly.

"You and your men want some grub?" Butter motioned to the fire pit. "We lost a couple of cattle in the fight. They won't keep, so we're eating right well these days. That is, if you like beef." He ran his tongue under his lower lip to worry loose a piece of stringy beef stuck between his teeth. Next he used the nail on his little finger. He got it, then spat.

"Boys!" Garrett called the men to eat while Tilman and the lawman sat apart, trying to sort out the last few days.

"Wagner, John Chisum looked me up to tell me you're David Stone's brother-in-law, and he speaks well of you both. As you know, Mr. Stone's been hurt and taken to his bed again, but he evidently trusts you to deliver his herd, so I reckon you've a right to know this. I've got a letter at the office from Governor Wallace. Seems David's boy Cam had been to see Wallace and told him about the situation with the rustlers."

"Well, I'll be." Tilman wiped his face with his bandana. "David loves that boy, and he was worried sick to think he'd gone over to the other side. That will make him feel a whole lot better. Any chance of a pardon?"

"Already done, Wagner. The governor offered the pardon for information, and Cam more than helped him get the goods on Stillwell and his gang. I have his pardon in Lincoln at the courthouse, but it's sealed, so nobody knows about it but us. He just needs to pick it up. Far as

I'm concerned, Cam's a closed case." Garrett stood. "I'm hungry. Let's eat."

After beef and coffee, Tilman told Garrett about Dunn. "Stillwell says that Franklin Dunn is behind everything. Apparently he not only cheated his partners but everyone he's come into contact with. He always made me uncomfortable. I think now I may have seen a warrant for him a couple of years back. Figure he left Texas, faded from view, and has now reestablished himself in the Territory."

"Guess he got greedy. Happens all the time. A man thinks he can get by with more, he does, then wants even more, and before long things come unraveled, and it's all caught up with him." Garrett snorted. "I'll tell you the rest of it. The governor said there's a deputy U.S. Marshal come to town with a paper on Dunn."

"Not a warrant!" Tilman said.

"It is. Some former land office clerk implicated Dunn in a fire that burned up a lot of old deeds and records in the Federal building. Dunn tried to have him rubbed out to keep him quiet, but something went wrong. The assassin's gun misfired, so the clerk threw a pot of boiling coffee at the fellow. Then he ran out the back door and hid in the dark down by the river. Next day the clerk made his way to the law in Albuquerque and swore out a complaint."

Garrett chuckled at the thought of what a picture the frightened man's hurried departure must have made. He stretched out one leg and rubbed a sore knee.

"Of course, there was more to it than that. It turns out Dunn cooked up a scheme to steal Spanish grant land here in the county that he claimed was never surveyed. Wouldn't you know, it was Stone's RD he'd set his sights on. Well, Dunn never had a legal leg to stand on. He twisted the Homestead law to suit him, counting on nobody asking questions, and those who did, his boys put under the sod." Garrett hitched up his gun belt. "One of the men he killed was a pard of mine, and I owe him for that." Garrett's eyes glinted with cold promise. "He'll pay. Well, I think I'll grab a few hours' sleep, then me and the boys will head back with Stillwell and the others to Lincoln. What are your plans? Are there enough of you to take the rest of the cattle to White Oak?"

"We'll be fine. Our herd is smaller, and we can handle it. Especially with Stillwell and Pickett out of the way. Should be back to Rocas Duras in a week."

"It was good meeting you, Wagner. Don't worry about Dunn. His days are numbered. I'll take care of him, and if I don't, why, the Deputy Marshal will."

"Garrett, I'm much obliged to you for telling me this."

Chapter Thirty-nine

Avoiding Garrett and his men, the old soldier called Sarge watched from a distance and later slipped away to ride to Dunn's ranch.

"I couldn't get close enough to spring Stillwell on account of they had a fellow guarding 'im. When I saw Garrett and his deputies talkin' to Wagner, why, I high-tailed it here. Didn't want no part of that."

Stillwell had proven to be worthless, and if Sarge hadn't found Dunn to tell him what had transpired, Dunn would probably soon be looking at life from behind a set of bars. Once Sarge got through with the woes of Pickett and his gang, Franklin knew his days in New Mexico Territory were numbered.

Paying Sarge off, Dunn sent him packing on his way to Tascosa to find Pickett or a new group of rustlers.

"Don't waste time. Get out of this country. I plan to head west, maybe to California."

"You want me to ride with you, Dunn?"

"No. I'm used to traveling by myself."

Sarge, wasting no time, left in a cloud of dust with nothing more than the clothes on his back and his payoff from Dunn.

Dunn packed a Gladstone bag, then went out and hitched a long-legged mare to his fancy surrey. After throwing in a few camp supplies—he had no time for anything else—he gathered up a couple of money belts filled with fifty gold double eagles he kept for emergencies. He'd be on his way to San Francisco soon enough, but first he had to make one final stop on the way. There was something in Socorro he wanted. He might not get Rocas Duras, but he intended to have Beatriz, one way or the other.

The next afternoon found Dunn in front of Santa Rosa Baca's home, admiring the wide front porch. The afternoon sun setting behind the large house caused the white gingerbread trim to take on a warm, rosy hue. It was quite a house, but it was only a house. Banker Baca had done well for himself, but he amounted to small change compared to what Dunn intended to amount to one day. No one seemed to be in the front, so Dunn made his way around to a side entry.

Inside he could see Beatriz and her sister, Graciela, sitting on a deep blue velvet love seat. Beatriz grew more beautiful each time he saw her. She needed taming, but he was just the man to do that. Then, as his wife, she would forget this life right quick. He would shower her with jewels and servants and all that she could ever need or want.

"Here, Graciela. Let me get Antonio. I hear him crying."

"You are going to spoil him, Beatriz." Graciela set her glass of sherry on a side table. "He is fine. Maria will bring him in here."

"I'll be right back." Beatriz left the room and went into the central hallway. Franklin didn't hesitate. He slipped through the open doorway and stood behind Graciela. Hearing a small noise, Graciela turned, a scream caught in her throat when she saw a man holding a gleaming silver derringer.

"Good afternoon, Mrs. Baca. How are you?" Dunn said conversationally as he came around the sofa to stand beside her. "I'm sorry I didn't knock, but I'm in a bit of a hurry."

"What are you talking about, Mr. Dunn?" Graciela's heart raced, her mind full of questions.

"Here we are—oh!" Beatriz stood in the doorway with Antonio in her arms. She froze as she saw the silver derringer pointed at Graciela. "Mr. Dunn, what are you doing? Let my sister go! Are you mad?" Antonio started to whimper, sensing that something was not right.

"Beatriz, listen carefully. I am perfectly sane. Now, be still, hand your nephew over to his mother, and then you and I are going for a ride." Dunn nudged Graciela with the gun. "No foolish theatrics, my dear. Just do as I say, and all will be fine."

Slowly Beatriz handed Antonio to Graciela and made her way to Dunn's side.

The only sound in the room came from Antonio, as he reached for the shining blue beads Graciela wore. "Mamá."

Beatriz backed up as Dunn held her arm, and they moved toward the open door. A tearful Graciela held Antonio, desperately afraid.

"Don't cry, Mrs. Baca." Dunn smiled, his eyes as cold as ice. "Tell your father that we'll be in touch with him as soon as we can. It's a long trip to California, and my bride-to-be and I may want to take our time to get to know each other better."

"Tell him yourself, Dunn!" Walter Krell stood behind Dunn, the long barrel of his shotgun cold on the back of Dunn's head. "It's in your best interest to let Miss Beatriz go and drop that gun. Now!" Krell pushed his rifle against Dunn. "We Germans aren't known for patience."

The gun dropped. Dunn frantically looked for a way out, only to see Baca and Socorro's hardcase sheriff bounding up the porch steps. The young boy he'd paid to take the message to Beatriz a few weeks before watched from the front gate.

"You!" he said to the boy.

"*Sí, señor.* I remember you from before." He grinned, obviously pleased with himself. "Señor Baca tell me he will pay well if I see you here again."

"Come along, Dunn." The sheriff handcuffed Dunn and turned to Krell. "Good work, son. You ever get tired of farming, come find me. I'll have a job for you in town."

Beatriz gazed at Walter with a mixture of admiration and surprise. "Walter, where did you come from?"

"It is a long story. However, your mother sent me to tell you and Graciela that she wants you all to come home." Walter looked to Señor Baca, who nodded in agreement.

Chapter Forty

Days later, Tilman and Butter were almost back to the RD.

"What in tarnation?" Butter pointed to the road. "If that don't beat all."

"What do you see, Butter?"

"I don't rightly know, Tilman, but yonder comes the Sheik of Araby!"

The two men, with James craning his neck to see also, looked at the odd sight coming up the road. As it got closer, they realized it was Walter Krell driving a buckboard, but not just any old buckboard. Brightly colored quilts and tasseled silk pillows lined the short bed, which was shaded by a lady's parasol. It appeared as if something or somebody lay bundled inside.

"If you fellows say one thing, I'll personally whip

you both. When I can, that is," came a man's voice from beneath the parasol.

David's head appeared from among the quilts as Walter turned in the driver's seat to watch.

"Mr. Wagner, the women made me bring him like this, and I couldn't argue with any of them." Walter helped David sit up as he looked at the riders circling the makeshift conveyance. The man winced, not quite healed.

"I'm fine, but Esperanza and the ladies thought I needed a little fresh air, and this is what we got. One of the boys spotted you about an hour ago and came to get us so we could at least finish the ride with you."

"Are you feeling better, David?" Tilman didn't quite know what to say. Where to begin? "Have you heard anything about Dunn?"

David pointed with his chin to Walter, saying, "This young man here captured Dunn in Socorro and held him until the sheriff took him off. It's a long story, but we'll talk about it over supper."

"I didn't do much, sir. When I saw Dunn with that gun and Beatriz in danger, my blood ran cold. I didn't think. I just acted." Walter blushed, trying to change the subject. "Mr. Wagner, did Sheriff Garrett get Stillwell and his boys?"

"Stillwell's in the lockup by now. After the Territory's done with him, he's a fugitive from Texas law and will go face the music there." Butter filled them in as they got ready to finish the ride. "That is, if that cough don't kill him first."

"Well, dang it, David. Aren't you curious as to how your cattle did?"

"Sure, I am. Now, tell us how the drive worked out. Are we broke?"

"Uncle David, Dad got top dollar for everything we brought in, plus a new contract for next year for you. What do you think of that?" James could contain himself no longer. "Oh, I'm sorry, Dad."

"That's okay, son. It beat anything we could imagine, David. Apparently some of the other drives came up short, so they were glad to get what we brought."

The men rode, Tilman curious about Cam and Juan Javier. "I talked to Garrett, and he said that Cam was acting under Governor Wallace's direction when he took a big risk to go back to the rustlers. Garrett said it was over as far as he was concerned."

"Well, it's a good thing about the boys. Maybe not the best way to come to know how much you need your brother and your family, but surely one that lasts."

Butter had been quiet, deep in thought. "When do they get home?"

"How about in a few minutes?"

Tilman, gun in hand, spun around, only to see Juan Javier's smile and the elusive Cam. He holstered the gun and wheeled his horse. "Cam." He held out his hand, choosing to ignore the previous meeting he'd had with this young man in Tascosa.

The men stopped so Cam could climb into the wagon with his father. Juan Javier guided his horse to the other side of the rig. They turned back toward the Rocas Duras.

"Butter. You old softy!" Tilman looked at his good friend, who brought out a worn and faded bandana and wiped his moist eyes. "Let's get this lash-up on the road. I bet Neala has doughnuts and Tomasa has green chile stew."

"Be quiet, Tilman. You're making my stomach rumble. Race you to the gate. It's time to be home." Butter let fly with a Rebel yell, slapped his horse, and started for the gate.

Epilogue

"Are you sure you all need to leave so soon?" Tilman watched as Butter loaded David's surrey and the packhorse. The last few weeks at David's had been full of a sense of reconciliation and renewal as Tilman and Butter helped the Stones get the ranch back into working order.

"Seems like we've hardly had time to visit, and now you're on your way back to Texas. You sure you two don't want to come to Colorado with us?" Tilman asked Butter.

Butter looked over at the rose garden, where Neala sat working on a small quilt in the shade of the trees, with Catherine and Esperanza keeping her company. "I'd like to stay, Tilman, but Neala and I are no youngsters, and she needs to get back to her brother's ranch, where she can rest. This has been rough on her. Besides, I like the country around there, and we'll do well. Colorado is a good place, but you, my friend, are a wandering man. I can't see you staying in one place for long. And somehow I don't think Catherine will mind tagging along wherever you go. Thanks just the same. When are you leaving?"

"I'm not sure yet. We thought we'd stay for a few more weeks and then decide." They both stopped talking as David and his sons rode up. The men had ridden out earlier in the day, and the three of them together was a sight to see.

"Think Cam is done with his wanderlust, Tilman?"

"Who knows? They've all come a long way the last few weeks. It won't be easy, but I think the fact that they almost lost David and Juan Javier made them all realize how short life really is. Cam knows what he put the family through, and I think he can see that the grass isn't necessarily greener on the other side of the fence. A lot of that green is plain old weeds. A person can't keep putting off making things right until something happens and it's too late to make amends."

The sound of Beatriz and Walter laughing inside the house drew their attention.

"I think there might be a wedding coming up in the next few months," Butter said.

Cam easily slipped off his roan barb. "Uncle Tilman, we have a telegram for you. The rider was heading this way, so we brought it."

"Don't you tell Catherine. Telegrams ain't never good news for Tilman here." Butter looked over Tilman's shoulder as he opened the note.

TILMAN STOP RETURN VISTA BUENA STOP I AM GETTING MARRIED STOP PASTOR FRY

Butter's Rebel yell carried far across the prairie.